F
Bannerman, Mark.
The frontiersman

THE FRONTIERSMAN

Frank Riddle flees from his tyrannical father and heads west to the Californian Gold Fields. But on the way, he encounters terrible Indian atrocity. At first, he hates and fears the Indians, but Fate deals him a strange hand when he takes a Modoc Indian woman as his squaw. His allegiances change, and he realizes that right is not always on the side of the whites. As the heavy-handed army moves in, Riddle fights not only to save lives but also to reconcile his own conscience.

MARK BANNERMAN

THE FRONTIERSMAN

Complete and Unabridged

LINFORD
Leicester

First published in Great Britain in 1999

First Linford Edition
published 2004

British Library CIP Data

Bannerman, Mark
  The frontiersman.—Large print ed.—
Linford western library
1. Western stories
2. Large type books
I. Title
823.9'14 [F]

ISBN 1–84395–127–4

Published by
F. A. Thorpe (Publishing)
Anstey, Leicestershire

Set by Words & Graphics Ltd.
Anstey, Leicestershire
Printed and bound in Great Britain by
T. J. International Ltd., Padstow, Cornwall

This book is printed on acid-free paper

This book is dedicated to the
treasured memory of my father
Major Herbert Charles Lewing

Cast of Main Characters:

Civilians

Frank Riddle	Army scout & interpreter
Ben Wright	Led massacre of Modocs
Alfred Meacham	Peace Commissioner
Rev. Thomas	Peace Commissioner
John Fairchild	Californian rancher
Donald McKay	Warm Springs Chief
Bernard Semig	Contract Surgeon
Thomas Cabbiness	Contract Surgeon

Army

Gen.ERS Canby	Commander, Dept of Columbia
Col Jeff C Davis	Successor to Gen Canby
Lt Col F Wheaton	Commander, 21st Inf
Col A Gillem	Successor to Col Wheaton
Major J Green	Field Commander
Major J Jackson	Commander Troop B
Capt E Thomas	4th Artillery

| Lieut F Boutelle | Company Officer Troop B |
| Henry McElderry | Assistant Surgeon, |

Modoc Indians

Captain Jack	Chief Lost River Modocs
Toby Riddle	Wife of Frank Riddle
Scarfaced Charley	Modoc Indian
Curly Headed Doctor	Modoc shaman
John Schonchin	Modoc Indian
Bogus	Modoc Bloodhound
Boston Charley	Modoc Indian
Hooker Jim	Modoc Bloodhound

1

It was July 1853. I was sprawled close to my lonely campfire, when distant gunfire bludgeoned the Californian night. My horse stopped munching the grass and raised his head in alarm. Fear of Indians quickened my breathing. I stood up and stamped out my fire.

I was a skinny eighteen but my beard was sprouting and folks took me for older. A year back I'd run off from home in Kentucky, scared Pa would trail after me and whip the skin from my back the way he'd done before. Had I not loved my mother so dearly, I'd have left ages ago. After she died there was nothing to stay for, and so I'd drifted west, lured by tales of gold in California. I'd crossed the Rockies at South Pass, and reached Fort Hall, then continued on through Thousand Springs Valley to the Humboldt River.

1

After that I'd crossed the Black Rock Desert and cut through Fandango Pass. I'd never realized country could be so big and downright lonely. There were times when I figured it would take the rest of my life to get across it.

Now, I listened to the gunfire, reckoning it was some five miles off. Presently it stopped.

I waited until daylight, then saddled my horse and rode forward, my rifle ready.

The country consisted of sage studded with junipers, the grass high enough to hide an entire Indian tribe. I went, scanning near and far, my spine tingling as I wondered if a man heard the swoosh of an arrow before it killed him.

Smoke tainted the air.

Skirting the butte, I reached the shore of a lake and I saw metal hoops jutting from the grass — wagons thrown on their sides. Only the metalwork was left, everything else was smoldering ash.

Dismounting, I crept forward.

I saw dead oxen lying in the grass, arrows jutting from them. Strewn about were ripped-open boxes, tin platters, kettles, clothing . . . and then I saw folks' bodies. Indians must have ambushed this wagon train, done their murderous work and vanished into the wilderness. Corpses of whole families lay together, their scalps torn away. Some folks had clearly tried to escape into the lake but the Indians had caught them and hacked them down.

I'd never seen people naked like this before. Naked, dead and bloody. It was like hell.

Suddenly something else caught my eye. A little girl, maybe six or seven years old, sitting on a rock. She looked pretty in her blue dress. As I hurried towards her, the truth dawned on me. I lifted her down. Her body was stiff, but there was no blood on her. She must have died of fright.

I scraped out a shallow grave, crossed her rigid arms over her chest and buried her. Hers was the only body I laid to rest. Don't ask me why, but she somehow seemed special. I should have said some Christian prayer over the grave, but I didn't because I felt in a daze.

I returned to my horse, mounted up. He was spooked and as anxious to move out as I was. I knew up ahead was a town called Yreka. I had to get there with word of the tragedy.

* * *

I reached Yreka two days later. The town as yet had no buildings, just numerous tents. Halfway up the main street was the biggest tent of all: *Wheelock's Saloon*, and from within came the sound of revelry. I hitched my horse and shouldered my way in, stepping over three drunks sprawled on the mud floor.

Leaning against the makeshift bar was a sad-eyed sheriff.

'Injuns hit a wagon train,' I told him.

'I found it two days back. Nothin' I could do.'

He swore, then started to shout and somehow he quieted the rabble. He nodded at me. 'You tell 'em, mister.'

So I did, sparing none of the bloody details. As I finished I could feel anger seething through the place and suddenly somebody shouted, 'Modocs done it for sure. Let's send for Ben Wright. He'll make them redskins pay for this!' and voices were yelling agreement.

Of course I didn't know who Ben Wright was, but he sounded awesome.

To my amazement I was hailed as some sort of hero and treated to whiskey. Soon I had a head that felt as if a chicken was trying to hatch from it, but come nightfall I'd managed to make camp on the edge of town.

Within two days, I'd bought prospecting gear and provisions, then I traveled to the diggings at Greenhorn Creek and staked myself to a fifty-foot claim, registering it with the owner of the saloon who kept a list of claims. 'Sure is rich pickin's along the creek,' he commented. 'One fella told me he plucked up some grass and there was gold-flakes glintin' in the roots!'

At Greenhorn Creek, the river flowed between tall pines. Hundreds of tents were pitched along the banks and miners were wading into the water with their sifting pans. Soon, I was doing likewise, straining my eyes for glint of gold. After three days, I got my first small success and thereafter I was truly smitten with gold-fever. The following Sunday I lined up at the assayer's office to have my pickings weighed. Afterwards, I heard that a burial party had gone out to the place where the wagon train had been ambushed.

That evening the fellow called Ben Wright stood on a platform in town. 'I want a hundred men to help me finish the Indians once and for all!' he shouted. 'The pay'll be good!'

Wright was a stubby man with glossy black hair hanging to his waist, and two ivory handled pistols were tucked into the belt of his buckskin suit. He was a real rabble raiser and by the way he told the story, you'd have figured it had been him who'd discovered the massacre.

He soon raised his men. Everybody was spoiling for Indian blood. Maybe I should have volunteered, but I didn't hanker to return to that place — and the lure of gold still drew me. So when Wright led his vigilantes out of Yreka, I returned to panning for gold.

As more miners flooded in, my life settled into a pattern. I went into partnership with three other fellas and we purchased a long-tom, a trough for washing gold from the gravel. The pay-dust we extracted didn't make us a fortune, but it was enough to keep us searching for more.

Meanwhile, Yreka was booming, tents being replaced with buildings as the population grew. I admit it: I went there to taste the sins on offer. I got liquored up, womanized and gambled away my earnings like most of the others.

It was late September when Wright led his vigilantes back into town. They were shaggy and bloodstained — but they were cock-a-hoop, firing their guns skywards. They had scores of Indian scalps dangling from their rifles. They even brandished fingers, noses and private parts they'd hacked from Indian bodies. The Modocs had come south to camp on Lost River, and the vigilantes had massacred them. 'We butchered Injuns just like they butchered them white folk,' one man boasted.

To Yreka folk, the vigilantes were heroes. Whiskey flowed and men took time off from mining and the town went on an almighty booze. Ben Wright had made his mark on history, and we reckoned that justice had been done, that the Modoc tribe had been taught a lesson and the Indian troubles were over.

Or so folks figured.

2

The next years brought many changes to my life. Having concluded I'd never make a fortune out of gold, I scraped together enough money to buy a cabin and land at Bogus Creek, twenty miles south of Yreka, and started a small-holding. I bought a few cows and over time developed my holding into a cattle spread.

Most of the Modoc Indians who survived the Ben Wright massacre went north and settled on a new reservation at Yainax. Gradually, as fresh folk populated the country, memories faded and some of the distrust between whites and reds died out. Later, many of the Indians even worked as laborers on ranches, though not mine. The mention of Modocs still sent shudders up my spine.

Modocs wore the cast-off clothing of

whites and generally behaved themselves, but one small band refused to live on the reservation. They camped at Lost River under their chief Captain Jack and sub-chief Hooker Jim, and lived peacefully enough, but some local ranchers didn't like Indians remaining 'wild'.

Captain Jack, so called because of his resemblance to a prospector of that name, sometimes visited Yreka. Apparently, his father had been killed in Ben Wright's attack. Now, in his late twenties, Jack was lithe and wiry. His face was broad and bronzed with high cheekbones, but it was his dark, watchful eyes that made people uneasy, because you wondered what thoughts were behind them. None the less, he earned some respect when a bakery in town caught fire and he helped in carrying children to safety.

★   ★   ★

My own biggest drawbacks were lonesomeness and the need for somebody to help with the chores.

One Sunday in Yreka, a Miss Bluebell, resplendent in feathered hat and red-rouged cheeks, climbed onto the saloon bar. She had her skirts hoisted so high you could see her legs all the way up to her silver-glinting garters. With hands on hips and legs astride, she proclaimed to the drinkers, 'Now listen here! If any fella wants a wife, with all the natural benefits, I'll serve for a year to the highest bidder!'

For a moment nobody said anything. Mouths opened but no words came out. A wife for a whole year . . . could this be true? At last a miner called Carver, who was eighty if he was a day, made a bid of $50, and that started off an avalanche of bidding, including mine which was soon overtaken. Eventually Miss Bluebell was snapped up for $500 in gold. The lucky winner carried her off in his arms amid hoots, cheers and crude advice.

Of course I envied him like everybody else did, never dreaming that my needs were to be met in a very different way.

On a May morning in 1860, an old Indian rode up to my cabin. Instinct warned me that he was a Modoc. He was leading a pony with a young girl astride its back. 'My daughter,' he said in English. 'Good price.'

'No,' I grunted, still suspicious of Modocs. 'I don't need a woman.' The last comment was totally untrue of course.

He just waited, blinking his droopy eyelids in the morning sunlight. I glanced at the girl. Two, wide brown eyes were suddenly twinkling at me and I noticed how the young buds of her breasts poked at her buckskin dress. Her hair was fixed in two long braids, and the parting along the center of her head was daubed with red ochre.

'Good worker,' the old buck said. 'Her name Nanook-to-wa. Captain Jack her cousin.'

'That doesn't make a grown woman out of this Nanook-eh, what's her name?'

The girl spoke for herself. 'Nan-ook-to-wa.'

There was no denying she was pretty. Maybe not all Modocs were bad. I'd seen other men take up with Indian women and they'd seemed to get on well enough.

'Three horses,' her father said.

I took a deep breath, then said, 'Two,' and after a moment he nodded.

I walked off and fetched two horses from my corral.

I was dazed with what I'd done. The girl was little more than half my size. She looked at me apprehensively, then she smiled, and I couldn't help but laugh and suddenly she laughed too.

The old buck gestured for her to dismount and touched her hair in a sort of farewell gesture, then he rode away, leading his new horses by a rope.

I returned to my cabin, and she followed me in. I wondered how we would make out. I hoped she'd prove a good worker. At least there would be no arguing. She couldn't understand English; I had no idea of Modoc. Later, I learned that her Indian name meant 'The Strange One' and only a month or so ago she'd undergone her tribal puberty rites.

As for me, I was twenty-five. I'd reckoned I was a doomed bachelor, and an Indian-hater. And now I was a squaw man. It didn't make sense.

* * *

That afternoon I took Nan-ook-to-wa to Yreka. I watched her eyes grow wide as she saw goods for sale in the stores — pretty dresses, shawls, bonnets — and she babbled excitedly in words I couldn't understand.

Ever since the massacre of the wagon train, the nearness of Indians had scared me. Now, here I was, feeling the crankiness easing from my soul, because one small Modoc girl was suddenly reminding me that life could be pleasing.

I bought her a yellow, long-skirted calico-dress and a set of beads.

I'd thought Indians were placid, never showing their feelings, but by golly I was wrong. My Modoc girl was as sure-fired thrilled as any white kid, and when we rode home she sucked happily on a candy-stick.

Once back at the cabin, I felt ashamed. It was a shambles of unmade bed, kicked over pail, dead whiskey bottles, dirty plates and pots. But her attention was on the package that contained her new dress. She unwrapped it, then drew her buckskin off over her head and she was naked. At that moment she shattered my ideas that she was a child. She was a young woman, fully fledged, with sweet, firm breasts and a smooth, dusky body.

She pulled on her new dress and smilingly twirled around for me to see. All I could do was nod.

I recalled that she didn't know my name — and hers was so tongue twisting I could hardly remember it.

'Me . . . Frank,' I said, pointing at myself.

'F-rank,' she nodded. 'Frank . . . '

And then I noticed how her eyes had drifted to an old Toby-jug on my shelf. It was a gaudy beer-mug, shaped like a man in a three-cornered hat. She took a shine to it and she lifted it down and held it in her hands, her round face full of puzzlement.

'Toby-jug,' I explained, and as she examined it, I returned to thinking about names. 'Me Frank, and you Nan-ook-eh . . . Oh it's too damned tongue-twisting! We'll give you a new name.' I rested my hand on her shoulder. 'You . . . Toby.'

She grinned. Maybe she didn't know I'd re-christened her, but she'd cotton on soon enough. And she looked real pretty in her yellow dress.

We soon got a fire started. She found the larder, what there was of it, and

16

soon rustled up a meal of beef, beans and rice.

Perhaps I should've been asking myself questions right then. Why had this girl moved in with me so suddenly? Maybe she was an Indian spy, preparing the way for her folks to come and lift my scalp.

That night I felt as woman-hungry as can be, but I still had the feeling in my head that Toby was just a kid — though I knew damned well she wasn't. I somehow didn't feel it was right to take advantage of her. But when I took to my blanket, she came and snuggled in against me, touching my beard with her fingers and making gentle, cooing sounds. Presently she rested her head on my chest. She went to sleep like a trusting, happily tired puppy. The warmth of her body seeped into my bones — and that was the way we spent the night.

Come morning when I awoke, she was outside, washing my clothes in the stream, and she spent the whole of the next day cleaning out and tidying the cabin. I watched bemused as she burned a small bundle of sage, spreading its smoky fragrance into every corner of the room.

As time passed, there were a lot of fellas who sniggered up their sleeves, but I didn't give a damn what they thought. I knew most of them had more to be ashamed of than me. The truth was that at the onset, me and Toby were more like brother and sister than anything else. I never touched my Indian squaw, like a man will touch his woman, for a whole week, but by then she was as randy as I was. 'Kiss, kiss,' she whispered into my ear as we snuggled together under our blanket. Apart from my name, those were the first English words she ever spoke. God knows where she learned them. She started to nibble my lips, but my beard tickled her and somehow she couldn't stop laughing.

After that, I won't deny we made up for lost time.

Before next winter set in, we'd strengthened the cabin and made it larger by building another room. Toby buckled into the work, sweeping and cleaning, airing the blankets. She helped with the stock and crops, did the cooking, sewed hides and made our clothes, washing them regularly in the stream.

She adapted to the white world well, flashing her smile at me whenever she figured I was looking. As she worked, she'd point at things and speak the Modoc words — a mixture of nasal and guttural sounds and clicking of the throat. *Mowich* was deer, *oumbo* was water; *U-Pi* was Horse Mountain. In turn, I taught her English words, and before long we were having small conversations — a mixture of Modoc, English and signs. We laughed together and sang. The Indian lingo was nowhere near so hard to learn as I'd reckoned.

In due course, I visited the Yainax reservation. This contained about sixty

Modoc families under an old chief. They lived in various bush wickiups and huts in wretched conditions, and I got to know many of them by sight and name. Their old enemies, the Klamath Indians, lived at the far end of the reservation on much better land. They always treated the Modocs as intruders. The Indian Agent, Alfred Meacham, supervised the entire reservation, doing his utmost to enforce a Christian way of life.

I was beginning to see Indians as real people, like the whites. They weren't just savage demons that appeared out of wild country to murder and pillage. They had feelings; they laughed; they cried. And maybe it was the whites that'd started the trouble in the first place by invading the country.

On one visit I learned something that shocked me: *It hadn't been the Modocs who'd massacred the wagon train. It had been a collection of warriors from other tribes.*

And so a few more years slipped by

and, with my Indian wife, I'd never been happier. Although Toby never forgot her Indian ancestry, she adapted to white ways, dressing like the ladies from town. She even took to riding her mare side-saddle.

Then one day trouble reared its head. An army courier arrived from the newly-erected Fort Klamath that was north of the Sprague River. The Commanding Officer was sending some soldiers to 'persuade' Captain Jack to take his people to the reservation. They wanted me to go along to interpret..

I hesitated, sensing that Jack would never agree to give up his freedom. But Toby reckoned I should go. 'Maybe you stop trouble starting,' she said.

I guessed she was right.

3

When we moved out from Fort Klamath, I went as civilian guide and official interpreter for the party. Major James Jackson, Lieutenant Boutelle and assistant Surgeon Henry McElderry led the column of thirty-five troopers.

That ride was misery. We rode through a wall of freezing sleet and my heavy canvas mackinaw stiffened with ice. For respite, we stopped at the town of Linkville, a small settlement of square-front stores and assorted cabins, which boasted forty residents, but today was as dismal as a cemetery.

As I warmed myself by the stove in the saloon, blowing on my steaming coffee, Lieutenant Boutelle joined me and said, 'I've heard a party of civilians somehow got word of our mission. Apparently, they started out for Lost River ahead of us. They intend to help us if things get rough.'

Boutelle was the most efficient and hard working officer I ever knew. He was a tall, handsome and slim man with a fine walrus mustache that he kept well groomed.

'I hope those civilians don't cause more trouble than they're worth,' I said.

Soon, Major Jackson had us moving again. He was a ruggedly built officer and right now he was ill with cramp in his guts, but he insisted on continuing. We were on that trail for sixteen wretched hours, and by early morning we were numb with cold. We followed along the foot of some low hills and at daybreak, we were within one mile of the Indian camp. The men were allowed to rest. Jackson beckoned Lieutenant Boutelle and me forward and we climbed a hillock and could see how the river flowed into the pale expanse of Tule Lake. There were Modoc wickiups on both sides of the river. Everything was weirdly silent, not an Indian or dog in sight. Captain Jack's village was on our side, while on the far side, I now recalled, was the village of the sub-chief Hooker Jim. In the loose Indian way, he was secondary to Jack.

Each wickiup was like a big upturned bird's nest and housed a whole family. They were fashioned from willow frameworks overlaid with tule matting and earth. A rough ladder up the side led to a hole in the top, which served as entrance, window and chimney.

'Wonder where those civilians are,' Boutelle remarked. 'Everything's so damned quiet down there.'

Jackson grimaced with his sickness. 'Do you reckon they know we're here?' he asked.

I shook my head. 'Jack probably figures only fools would be riding in this weather.'

'Well, I figure we should advance on his village.' Boutelle said.

'We've got to give them the chance to surrender before we attack,' I insisted.

We returned to the men. Carbines were made ready and we rode towards

Jack's village. We halted some twenty yards from the first wickiup. Half the force dismounted, handed their horses over to the remainder and formed a skirmish line. I kept close to Major Jackson as we moved forward and halted.

I glimpsed a movement beyond a wickiup to our left. Jackson opened his mouth to speak, but suddenly a shot cracked into the eerie hush. The sound had come from the direction of the river, and as all eyes swung that way we saw a Modoc with a red bandanna on his head. He was a young Indian who'd I'd once met at Yainax. An injury, slashing his cheek from forehead to jaw, had left his face lop-sided. His name was Scarfaced Charley. He had paddled his canoe across to our side of the river and was climbing the bank. He seemed to have stumbled. His gun had slipped from his grasp and gone off as it hit the ground. As he recovered the weapon, he saw the soldiers and he shouted in alarm.

Some warriors at the far end of the village climbed from their wickiups and gazed at us.

At that moment Jackson seemed at a loss. I cupped my hands to my mouth and shouted as loud as I could. 'Tell Jack to come out so we can talk. The soldiers will not harm you if you obey!'

Suddenly we heard a blast of gunfire from across the river. I had forgotten about the civilians who had come on ahead of us. Now it was clear that fighting had broken out in Hooker Jim's village.

'Lay down your guns and there'll be no trouble,' I yelled again in Modoc.

'The soldiers kill us — like Ben Wright kill us!' Scarfaced Charley shouted back.

More warriors had appeared, waving guns.

Jackson snapped out an order: 'Mister Boutelle, disarm Scarfaced Charley.'

Boutelle drew his revolver. He stepped forward. 'Give me your rifle,

Injun,' he shouted loudly. 'Give it here, you red son-of-a-bitch!' His language was loud, but his intention was to distract the Modoc for the seconds he needed to get in close and grab the gun.

Scarfaced Charley pointed his rifle. 'Me no dog!' he screamed, and pressed the trigger. The lieutenant also fired. Both shots missed.

A crowd of Indians had grouped about thirty yards to the front of the skirmish line. Jack had not appeared. Nor had the women and children. I guessed they were lying flat on the ground within the lodges, so as to be safe from bullets.

Modoc lead scorched through the air. Jackson shouted, 'Fire!' and his men opened up.

The Modocs scattered, finding cover behind the lodges and in the thick sagebrush to our left, firing as they went. The soldiers were exposed and, to my dismay, several went down. To add to the confusion, the army horses, which had been held at the edge of the village, burst free and stampeded amongst us.

Next to me, a trooper spun around, half his head shot away. I was briefly aware of his blood splattering across my face, but simultaneously I saw a Modoc kneeling down, taking aim at me with his bow. I lunged to the side, felt the *thrum* of an arrow brush my ear.

Jackson, realizing that we were too exposed, gave the order to fall back. A corporal yelled with agony and collapsed against my legs. Blood was soaking his shirt. A sergeant helped me drag him along as we retreated to where our first platoon had taken up position slightly back from the village. Meanwhile, soldiers were striving to round up the stampeding horses.

Doctor McElderry went to work on the wounded, and Jackson was reforming the skirmish line, shouting to establish order. Soon soldiers were pouring a fierce fusillade at the Modocs.

For several minutes the Indians returned the fire. Then they retreated in sudden flight, moving towards the south.

As the gunfire subsided, Jackson beckoned me over. 'We've killed quite a few of them,' he said. 'I haven't seen Jack, have you?'

I shook my head. I felt sickened. The whole thing had got out of hand and I'd failed to prevent bloodshed.

But Jackson's eyes reflected satisfaction. 'I figure this'll be the end of the trouble. Now we'll burn the village.'

'There's still families in the wicki-ups!' I shouted.

'All right. Tell 'em they've got five minutes to get out.'

So I stepped out from the covering sagebrush. The shooting had died out. Even from across the river, there was now no sound. I wondered what had happened there.

I yelled into the wind, hoping that the sheltering families would hear my warning. They did. Seconds later there was a nervous scurrying from the wickiups. Women, some carrying children, emerged, glancing apprehensively around, then they hurried towards the south where their men folk had gone. I wondered where Jack was.

The Modocs must have planned for such an emergency because they had canoes hidden among the tules on the riverbank, and soon they were paddling towards Tule Lake, fighting the wind and rain. *Please God*, I thought, *may the killing be finished*.

Jackson ordered his men to burn the village. Within ten minutes the wickiups were ablaze, dark black smoke swirling up into the wind. As for me, I felt that I'd betrayed Jack's Modocs. I'd been part of the force that had attacked them and destroyed their village, though I was certain that the Modoc casualties had not been so many as Jackson figured.

Doctor McElderry had set up a temporary first-aid post in the sagebrush. A dead private lay covered by a blanket. A corporal, shot through the lungs, was in a pitiful state and some of the others were also in a bad way. I fetched them water in a canteen.

Down at the river, some Indian canoes had been captured. It was agreed the wounded would be sent across the river in these and taken to Crawley's cabin that was to the west. Jackson would lead one platoon of men north and make the crossing at a point called Natural Bridge, and Boutelle and ten men would remain as rearguard in case any Modocs returned.

I went into the canoes with the wounded. 'You don't reckon they'll cut my leg off, do you?' a young private asked me. A bandage around his knee was sodden with blood.

'No,' I said and I prayed I was right.

4

Dennis Crawley's cabin had earth piled against the outside walls to keep out the cold. The place was a welcome sight as I ran the mile from our landing point on the river. I'd left Doctor McElderry tending the wounded. Help would be needed from Crawley's to convey the wounded to the cabin. About a mile off across the meadow, I could see the Modoc wickiups of the second village. Everything was hazed by smoke from Captain Jack's burning village.

As I approached the cabin, I heard shouting. Glancing to my right, I saw several mounted Modocs a quarter-mile distant and knew they'd spotted me. Fortunately, gunfire from the cabin made them turn their horses away. With relief, I reached Crawley's open door.

Inside were a dozen grim-eyed settlers. The whole place smelt of guns, oil — and sweat, despite the cold. In the center of the room, sheltered beneath the table, were the two toddlers, their mother huddled alongside. The cabin was truly forted-up, ready for siege.

'We ferried wounded soldiers across the river,' I panted out. 'The doc needs help to get them up here.'

A quick conference was held and soon a group of six men left the cabin to assist Doctor McElderry.

Meanwhile, Dennis Crawley sighed loudly. 'This whole dawgone affair is a mess. Those Modocs will most likely reform and attack us.'

'Jackson and his soldiers should show up soon,' I commented, accepting a mug of coffee from Mrs. Crawley. 'We'll be safe then.'

I recognized a rancher called Applegate and realized that he'd led the civilians who had attacked the second village. 'What happened this side of the river?' I asked him.

'A crowd of ranchers decided to help the army. They've been campaigning to get the Modocs off this land for years. I tried to keep things low-key, but it was hopeless.'

I nodded. I didn't trust him. He wanted the Modocs off this land as much as anybody.

'At dawn,' Applegate continued, 'when we realized the soldiers were moving into Jack's village, we followed suit on the west side. I got talking to Hooker Jim. I tried to persuade him to surrender, but it was no good. Shooting started and Jack Thurber got killed. Mind you, some Modocs got hit too. They took cover behind their lodges, but we were in the open, so we had to get out quick. They chased us, firing all the time. We made it back to this cabin and forted-up. That wasn't long before you got here.'

A thought occurred to me. 'Have the settlers north of Tule Lake been warned? Seems they could be mighty vulnerable.'

'Sure,' Applegate said. 'One-Armed Brown rode to tell 'em to watch out.'

Soon we could see the men approaching from the river, struggling with make-shift stretchers. Thankfully, the Indians didn't trouble them. Doctor McElderry had his patients brought into the cabin and Mrs. Crawley tried to comfort the sufferers, but within minutes, the corporal who had been shot through the lungs gasped the words, 'Sweet Jesus,' and died.

I reckoned Jackson should be here by now.

I went outside. The light was fading and the weather was as bad as ever. There was no sign of Jackson's column.

I figured Jackson had been wrong when he'd claimed the Modocs were finished. The raid on Lost River had stirred up a hornets' nest. Jack himself hadn't been seen, but I guessed he'd somehow escaped.

In the cabin we waited to see what would happen. The Modocs didn't seem in any hurry to rush us, but the general opinion was that it would be foolhardy to leave Crawley's.

Eventually Jackson's bedraggled column appeared, bringing some horses they'd rounded up, including mine. As the soldiers rode into Crawley's, Jackson himself looked at Death's door.

'No sign of any Modocs,' he gasped, 'but the water was so damned high, we couldn't use the ford. We had to go seven miles upstream to do the crossing.'

Later that evening, Lieutenant Boutelle and his men arrived. The Modocs hadn't attempted to return to what was left of the eastern village. 'Seems they crossed Tule Lake towards the Lava Beds,' Boutelle told us. 'As for Hooker Jim and the rest from the western village, they seem to have disappeared.'

It was near midnight when a shout went up from our guards. I'd been trying to sleep, wrapped in a blanket. I scrambled up and stepped outside. One of the soldier-guards was holding up a lantern and a horseman rode up and slid from his saddle — a bulky figure in a black cape. This was One-Armed Brown.

Brown reported to Boutelle, then he came into the cabin.

'Did you warn all the homesteads?' I asked him, thinking particularly about Bill Brotherton who was an old friend of mine.

'Yeah,' he nodded, extracting a plug of baccy from his jaw with his finger. 'They're all forted up now. I reckon I've earned some shut-eye.'

He drank some coffee, then bedded down on the floor. I returned to my own blanket and dozed off. I was awakened by the changing guards. It was getting lighter. A thought gnawed at me. I rose to my feet, moved over to where One-Armed Brown was snoring. A nudge brought him to belligerent wakefulness.

'Did you go to the cabins north of Tule Lake?' I asked.

He swore. 'Didn't know there was any settlers up there.'

'Damn it!' I snapped. 'That's just

where the Modocs are likely to hit.'

Brown snorted. 'Well, I ain't paid to go runnin' after dawgone settlers!'

I found Major Jackson. He was talking to the guards outside the back of the cabin where our horses had been corralled. I told him that the settlers along the north side of the lake hadn't been warned.

'Well I can't spare my men to carry word,' he said. 'If you figure those folks need warning, you best do it yourself.'

I nodded. I found my horse amongst the remuda, got him saddled and rode out. I figured I might be too late.

★ ★ ★

Two hours later, I was riding through high sagebrush when I heard gunshots. Earlier, I'd reached the Boddy cabin, but it was locked up and deserted. Now, I quit the sagebrush, and before me stretched meadowland. On this was the cabin of the Brotherton family. On the intervening ground, I saw a horseman galloping away from a flock of sheep. And, then, appearing from the high sage, more horsemen appeared, pursuing the first rider. They rode at him from an angle, firing their rifles. The first rider dropped from his horse. He was a German called Nicholas Schira, a sheepherder who worked for the Brothertons, and his attackers were Modocs. One of them had dismounted, was scalping the unfortunate Schira — Hooker Jim!

Suddenly the Modocs were shouting, heads turning as a small figure appeared, racing towards the Brotherton house on foot. It was Joseph the young son of Bill Brotherton. The Modocs surged after him like wolves.

I heeled my mount towards the running boy, at the same time unsheathing my rifle. I was angling in directly between the Modocs and the boy. The Modocs hesitated as they saw me. From the right, the crack of a gun sounded. Mrs. Brotherton had emerged from the cabin brandishing a rifle. I raised my gun and fired. The bullet went yards wide, but the Modocs swung away.

I reached Joseph and hauled him up behind me, and a moment later we reached the woman. I reined in my animal, and we slid from its back, and ran into the cabin.

Mrs. Brotherton shut the door and drew bolts across. Also in the room was Joseph's eight-year-old brother, Charley.

Mrs. Brotherton swung round, her gray hair awry. 'Why're the Modocs doing this?' she shouted.

'There's been a fight between Injuns and soldiers. The Modocs are out for revenge.' I glanced around the room, saw some sacks of flour. 'Stack them against the door,' I gasped. 'They'll probably try to rush us.'

While the Brothertons dragged the sacks into position, I peered through the window. The Indians were waving their guns in the air, screaming defiance.

I saw Hooker Jim gesture, and they kicked their animals forward in a charge. Both Mrs. Brotherton and I opened fire with our rifles, blasting off wildly. One Modoc went down but he was up instantly, mounting behind another Indian.

Our fire discouraged them and soon they drew back out of range.

'Where's your husband?' I asked Mrs. Brotherton.

'He went out to collect wood. I hope the Modocs ain't found him.' She glanced at me, her eyes wild. 'I knew we could never trust them Injuns. They should've been wiped out years ago.'

I said, 'My woman is a Modoc. Some Modocs are as good as whites.'

She didn't respond.

'Ma,' her younger boy Charley said, 'I'm hungry. When we gonna eat?'

'When your pa comes home,' his mother replied.

I'd been watching the Indians through the window.

Suddenly they started blasting away

with their guns, unleashing their vengeance on the sheep, cutting them down in a hail of lead.

'How many bullets have you got?' I asked.

She sighed. 'I guess we're real short. Bill took his rifle with him. Mister . . . do you figure the Injuns got him?'

'Just keep praying,' I said.

But her mind moved on. 'They'll wait till dark, then burn us out.'

'Maybe I should go for help.' I said, thinking aloud.

'They'd cut you down in no time,' she said. 'For God's sake don't leave us!'

Our situation was desperate, but now the light was beginning to fade. I tried to reason things out. Maybe killing us didn't matter to those Indians, but our resistance must have irked them. We should have been easy targets on which to avenge yesterday's violence.

We crouched, looking out the windows. Mrs. Brotherton gripped her gun in one hand and a large bread-knife in the other. Joseph was taking his turn as look-out. The younger boy was huddled beneath the table.

'Where's Bill?' Mrs. Brotherton murmured. 'I wish he'd come home.'

'Maybe he's gone for help,' I said, trying to lift our spirits.

Darkness deepened. Rain thudded on the roof and the younger boy began to cough.

Then we heard the pound of hooves approaching.

'God preserve us!' Mrs. Brotherton gasped.

I wondered if we should surrender ourselves, try to reason with them. But then I thought of Hooker Jim's harsh, hate-filled features, and I dropped the idea.

Suddenly, amid the thump of hooves, came another sound — the jingle of harness. The Modocs had been riding bare-back.

'That's not Injuns!' I gasped.

A voice came: 'Is anybody home? It's Lieutenant Boutelle from Fort Klamath!'

Mrs. Brotherton struck a match, lit a lantern, which she held up, and with overwhelming relief we cleared the barricade from behind the door. We watched the black hulks of soldiers and horses appear, halting in front of the porch.

'We thought you were Modocs,' I said as Boutelle dismounted and stepped into the light, wiping the rain from his fine mustache.

'No,' he grunted, 'but they've left a trail of blood. They've burned three homesteads, killed the men folk, run off their cattle.'

Mrs. Brotherton said, 'My husband went out yesterday. Ain't been back.'

'Where'd he go?' Boutelle enquired uneasily.

'To the junipers north o' here . . . '

'Mrs. Brotherton . . . I'm afraid we've got bad news. We found a body in the woods. It's strapped on a horse at the rear of the column.'

We walked along that line of grim, rain soaked troopers, the lantern raised.

A sergeant pointed to a blanket-shrouded hulk on a horse's back, and pulled the cover aside. We saw a patch of naked skull where the scalp had been torn away. Here was Bill Brotherton, no mistaking.

Mrs. Brotherton stood there, not making a sound, and presently her boys joined her. The sergeant replaced the blanket.

'You've got to come with us,' Boutelle was telling her. 'We'll return to Crawley's cabin. There are more soldiers there. You'll be safe.'

She reluctantly agreed and soon, with her boys, was helped into a springboard wagon, which had been brought up.

I said to Boutelle: 'I need a horse. Mine bolted in the fight. I want to get back to Yainax.'

'That's dangerous country. Modocs are roaming over it.'

'I know that, but I want to go.'

He was anxious to move off. 'We rounded up a few animals,' he shrugged. 'Help yourself and be on your way.'

I grunted my thanks, and five minutes later I was riding away from the army column and the bereaved Mrs. Brotherton.

5

After a wearisome ride I reached Yainax and reported my news to the Indian Agent Alfred Meacham. He was a short, stocky man with a bald head, a squarish face decorated with graying side-whiskers and mustache. Rumor had it that his ancestors were Quakers on the one side and Methodists on the other. My grim story had him grinding his teeth against the stem of his briar pipe.

'I suspect by now, Hooker Jim has joined Jack,' he gasped. 'Do you know the Lava Beds, Mister Riddle?'

'I've been there,' I responded. 'It's a God-forsaken place, a mass of volcanic rocks and caves.'

Meacham frowned. 'This is exactly the situation I've worked so hard to avoid.'

I nodded, leaving him looking

unusually crestfallen. He had a genuine respect for the Indians and a desire to maintain peace for all.

There followed a strange period of waiting. The weather worsened, with snow blocking the trails, and wild rumors spread through the Yainax agency. The agency Indians were in an agitated state.

One afternoon Meacham beckoned me into his office.

'The army's been reinforced,' he said, tamping baccy into his pipe-bowl. 'Patrols are combing the Tule Lake area and Jackson's still at Crawley's place.'

'I hear tell,' I chipped in, 'that the Governor of Oregon is raising a force of volunteers.'

'Everything's stacked against Jack,' Meacham said. 'If he doesn't see sense now, he never will.'

Later that day, a scout reported more news. Jack had made a stronghold in the caves on the southern shore of Tule Lake. It was a sacred place. He had been stocking it up with supplies for years, believing one day he would need sanctuary there. As we had expected, Hooker Jim and his marauders had joined him.

The following week, Toby and I were in Yreka. I bought a newspaper and read the column on the front page.

As the army's build up continues in the territory, rancher John Fairchild and some of his friends entered the Lava Beds. They met the Modoc chief Captain Jack in his stronghold. Jack stated that he could not understand why the soldiers had attacked his camp at Lost River. He considered that he had done nothing wrong. All he wanted was to be left in peace. He refused to go back to the Yainax Agency. He said he did not want war, but if the soldiers came after him he would fight. John Fairchild told our correspondent that the Modoc Stronghold was the most perfect, natural fortification he'd ever seen. The Modocs have meat from cattle they have stolen, and they will be self-sufficient. It is the opinion of many local persons, that the army must bring matters to a conclusion by applying sufficient force to compel the said Indians to submit.

In early January a new soldier-chief came to the area. Colonel Frank Wheaton set up his headquarters at Van Bremer's ranch. A ring of military posts had been established around the Lava Beds and word spread that a big attack was being planned to wipe out Jack and his followers.

Toby and I traveled down through the snowy, cold land. Late in the afternoon, we approached the scattered ranch-buildings of the Van Bremers. On the surrounding land, the whiteness of army tents and campfires showed. We were challenged by a sentry and allowed to cross the picket line and soon found the colonel's bell-tent. Another sentry stopped us but soon we were motioned to enter.

Wheaton was sitting at his command desk, huddled in his greatcoat. He had sharp, sensitive features and was studying the maps spread before him. He spoke in a raspy voice and he kept fingering his throat.

'Pleased to meet you, Riddle. I hear you've done good work for the army.' He paused, attempting to swallow. 'I've got damn quinsy and a throat-full of pus. Doctor said I should be in bed, but I haven't the time. Everybody's screaming for Modoc blood.'

'Colonel,' I said, 'my wife and I figure it might help if we pow-wowed with Jack before any attack is made. We might be able to talk him into giving up.'

Wheaton shook his head. 'No time. The territory is in a state of terror. I have orders to storm the Modoc stronghold. If they don't surrender, they're to be destroyed. Jack started this trouble. He's been given plenty of chances, but he refuses to go to Yainax. If we don't crush him, the Indians'll start another blood-bath.'

Wheaton suffered a bout of coughing. Another man had entered the tent. 'You sent for me, Colonel?' he said.

Wheaton nodded. 'Doc . . . I can't swallow. I want the swelling in my throat lanced before it drives me insane!'

The doctor opened up his bag and laid out his instruments.

I could see we were achieving nothing. 'Thanks, Colonel,' I said, 'I hope you feel better soon.'

Wheaton said, 'I'd appreciate if you come with us tomorrow. We may need you as interpreters.'

I nodded, grasped Toby's hand and we left the tent.

As we walked through the camp, we could sense that every soldier was anxious to get the job done. There were over three hundred regulars encamped here — and facing them, just fifty ill-equipped Modoc warriors and their families.

But there was something the soldier-boys hadn't taken into consideration. Fog.

★ ★ ★

Next morning the entire command was formed up in column of fours, and as Wheaton gave the order to move out, flank and rearguards spread wide.

We crossed over the sloping plateaus east of Van Bremer's and arrived on top of Sheepy Ridge in mid-afternoon. This overlooked the Lava Beds. Perry's troop awaited us. Equipment was unloaded, picket lines were set up and tents erected.

I gazed down the steep slope towards the area across which tomorrow's attack would be launched. All I could see was fog. It completely blanketed the ground.

A corporal, staggering under the weight of an ammunition box, joined me. He rested down his burden.

'This place gives me the creeps,' he

complained. 'Where d'you figure the Injuns are, mister?'

I pointed to the northeast. Their Stronghold's about three miles away,' I said, 'completely blotted out by fog.'

Suddenly he stiffened to attention as Colonel Wheaton came striding up. The officer seemed to have recovered from his throat trouble. 'The Modocs can fight or run,' he said. 'We'll finish 'em either way. We've just got to advance across that stretch of flat country till we link up with Bernard's men coming from the east.'

'That land isn't flat, Colonel,' I said. 'The fog hides crevasses and sharp rocks. The Injuns'll be able to fire on the troops from cover.'

'The fog will conceal us, Riddle. We'll be into their rocks before they realize what's hit 'em.'

As darkness took hold, the temperature dropped. I learned that civilian volunteers were camped at the base of the bluff, ready to link with the rest of the command in the morning. Soldiers warmed themselves around sagebrush fires, talking in subdued voices.

Reveille was called at 4 A.M.

Men gathered up their weapons and proceeded on foot down the steep face of the bluff, the cavalry being employed as foot soldiers.

It was still dark and freezing cold, and several times rifles were dropped, causing an awful clatter. It was a good hour-and-a-half before everyone was on the flat swale at the bottom, and the link was made with the civilian volunteers.

I watched as noncoms, their gritty voices hushed, got their men into formation. In the fog, they could hardly see more than an arm's length ahead of them.

I had no intention of joining in the battle, but I hung round Wheaton's field-headquarters, still hoping for some chance to prevent conflict.

Wheaton noticed me and beckoned me over. 'You wanted a final chance to speak to Jack.' His voice was getting husky again. 'I'll give you that chance. I'd like you to go out there and announce in as loud a voice as you can, that the Indians in the Stronghold have ten minutes to surrender or they'll face the consequences.'

The prospect of stepping out there, with bucks like Hooker Jim looking for targets, sent shivers up my spine, but all at once I heard my voice say, 'I'll go.'

Wheaton gave me a grateful pat on the back.

A moment later I was scrambling forward through the murk. I passed the outer line of soldiers, telling them what I was going to do.

The ground was rugged and I stumbled over a chunk of lava but went on.

You're a damned fool, I told myself. I suddenly felt awful lonesome in no-man's land, the cold knot of fear gnawing at my belly. I glanced ahead, but all I could see was fog. I continued, my legs feeling leaden. Presently, I heard the metallic click of a rifle, so I pulled up, figuring I was as near to the Modoc position as I was going.

I cupped my hands to my mouth and yelled in my loudest voice. I gave them Wheaton's ultimatum, then crouched down and listened. I got the exact answer I'd foreseen — silence. It seemed an age I waited, expecting at any second the blast of gunfire. But bullets never came, though presently something else did — a voice. It was scarcely a whisper, yet it was so chillingly close that it was totally audible.

'Go home, you sonovabitch. If you stay here, you die!'

I glanced around. I was wrapped in a blanket of fog. Somehow I found the nerve to speak. 'If you fight, many Modocs will suffer. You can't win. If you give up, nobody'll get hurt.'

My voice trailed off, and a response came — a stream of abusive cursing.

I didn't delay any longer. I circled back, sick that my last-ditch attempt to bring peace had been a failure.

When I was again with Wheaton, I related my disappointing news. 'Thank you, Riddle.' he said. 'You're a brave man.' He swung to his adjutant. 'The artillery is to open fire. Three shots. That's the signal to start the battle.'

Within a minute the howitzers roared, the hard smell of cordite tainting the air, and men were ordered to form a skirmish line and advance. Soon rifle fire sounded, though I was sure the only thing those soldiers were firing at was fog.

It was frustrating for us, knowing that conflict was going on yet unable to see a thing. At last dawn broke, but the fog remained thick. The gunfire continued, and as runners came back to Wheaton's field-headquarters it was obvious that morale was sinking fast. The Indians were making full use of their rocky cover, firing down on the advancing line.

'You were right, Riddle,' Wheaton presently admitted, staring into the murk. 'We were counting on howitzer fire to support the advance, but we better not open up because we'd probably hit Bernard and his men, wherever they are. This damned fog has done us no favors.'

I admired Wheaton. He had the guts to admit he'd been wrong.

Later, a runner arrived from the eastern flank and handed a dispatch to Wheaton. He read it, then turned to a major standing next to him, scowling. 'Bernard advanced this morning, but came upon a gorge. His men refused to cross, so they've halted and contented themselves with shooting in the direction of the Indians.'

The major nodded. 'I'm sure some of those shots are going over the Modocs and landing amongst our infantry.'

Wheaton said, 'I'm going forward to find out what's happening.' Shortly he and his group of staff officers moved out.

As the morning dragged by, the sound of Modoc voices bounced through the fog as they screamed insults at the soldiers.

Shortly after noon, Wheaton came back, cursing the fact that the Oregonian Volunteers had withdrawn. 'One of their men was killed,' he said, 'and the others turned tail.'

In early afternoon, with the fog still thick, Major Green, commanding the west side, sent word to Wheaton that he was under heavy fire and could progress no further. Wheaton ordered Green to circle around the back of the Modoc Stronghold, along the narrow strip of land between the rocks and the lake. That way, a link could be made with Bernard's force.

At three o'clock, a dispatch arrived stating that Green and his men had succeeded in passing along the northside of the Stronghold, but they'd been badly exposed and subjected to heavy fire, wounding Lieutenants Perry and Kyle and killing several enlisted men. Later I heard the firing was so intense that men cowered down, refusing to advance further. Green himself had climbed onto a rock, ignoring Indian bullets, urging his men forward. They'd made no effort to hold the lakeshore, but moved along and finally joined up with Bernard's concealed riflemen. In truth, little had been gained.

Back at the field-headquarters, I watched the dismal stream of wounded coming in. One of the Californian Volunteers had been shot in the head, but he was still on his feet. Meanwhile, Wheaton acknowledged that the situation was getting desperate. His men had had no decent rest for nearly forty-eight hours. Their uniforms, boots and skin had been ripped to bits as they'd crawled over the razor-sharp lava. They were hungry and cold, scared and beaten and their estimation of the Modocs had changed from contempt to awe.

I think it was about six o'clock, getting dark again, when the battle ended. Everybody seemed to have had enough and the sickened Wheaton wasn't arguing. 'Getting Indians out of that Stronghold,' I heard him admit, 'is like trying to get ants out of a sponge.'

He'd sure changed his tune.

Nobody had expected such a crushing defeat. There were no stretchers available and scant few medical orderlies. I went out to lend a hand as the wounded were laid on blankets and men hoisted the corners onto their shoulders and staggered forward. In the scramble back towards the bluff, there was a panicking fear that the Modocs would chase up behind.

'We've left some of our dead and dyin' back there!' a man cried out, waving a hand towards the battlefield.

'Well, we ain't goin' back,' somebody responded. 'That's for sure!'

Everything was in awful disarray. Many wounded were bumped roughly against the rocks and they cried out in agony, but nobody stopped to comfort them.

One man had his leg shattered by a bullet, his trouser leg sodden with blood. I found a mule and helped him onto its back. His injured leg dangled down and kept striking the rocks, making him yell with pain. Somebody found a rope and fixed it around his ankle like a pulley, so he could raise the limb clear of the rocks. As I tried to help him, I was almost knocked over by another mule as it charged past me. An officer was clinging to its tail, so exhausted that he was relying on the animal to drag him along.

As we grouped at the base of the bluff, word spread that Modocs were on top, setting an ambush for us as we scrambled up. Officers ordered their men to start the climb, but nobody would go. I'd left Toby on the ridge. I knew some Modocs would be mad at her because of the belief that she was helping the whites, but I didn't think they'd do her harm — even so, I was worried about her. Wheaton asked me if I would climb the bluff to check if it was safe, and he gave me a flare-gun to fire if all was well. So I clambered up the steep slope. It took me twenty minutes. Thankfully, I found Toby at our tent where I'd left her and I panted out what had happened.

'No Modocs up here, Frank.' she said. 'They all too busy killing sojers down below.'

I nodded, then fired the flare, and at last the shattered command deemed it safe to start the climb.

And that was how the fiasco ended. Afterwards, Wheaton tried to scale down its importance, calling it a 'forced reconnaissance'. Eleven soldiers had been killed, thirty wounded and countless more lacerated by the rocks.

Three hundred men had been routed by devilish terrain, fog and Indian know-how.

6

The throb of drums sounded and a huge victory fire, glowing from the Modoc stronghold three miles away, lighted the sky. It was midnight and I was with Wheaton, listening as the reasons for the disaster were argued over by distraught officers.

Only with first light did the drums cease.

Doctors had set up a tented hospital on the bluff, preparing the injured for the journey to Fort Klamath. One man suddenly screamed, then quieted.

The fog had now vanished and the army camp went through the motions of military routine. Men hobbled to their breakfast. Some could hardly walk, they were so bruised from the rocks.

Suddenly a cry sounded from the lookouts and breakfast was immediately forgotten. Men gazed down from the ridge, perhaps getting their first clear view of the terrain. Its tortured rock, giant cinders, peaks and craters were darkened by ugly black lava spewed out by ancient volcanoes.

In the far distance, Peninsula Rock stood like a watchful sentinel, but nearer, hidden in a depression, was Jack's Stronghold, its presence now betrayed only by campfire smoke.

'See,' a man shouted, pointing. 'There's goddamned Injuns down there.'

An officer was standing beside me. He was Major Green who had been in the thick of battle yesterday. He was a heavy-featured man with a black beard. 'Modocs — men and women,' he said. 'They're scavenging the battlefield for weapons we abandoned yesterday . . . and no doubt murdering any wounded they find.'

A flurry of oaths sounded, but no order was given to go out to engage the enemy.

It was two more hours before Wheaton dispatched a detail down onto the battlefield. By now the Indians had returned to the Stronghold, taking their spoils with them — guns, ammunition, clothing. They left behind them the stripped remains of dead soldiers.

The Indians made no attempt to molest the recovery detail. Later that morning, guards stood watchful as the bodies were buried at the base of the bluff. Colonel Wheaton was greatly distressed by the loss of his men.

Presently he issued orders. 'We're falling back to Van Bremer's ranch. Captain Bernard's command will return to Louis Land's ranch. Riddle, I'll offer you good wages if you'll act as official guide.'

'I'm not going to fight the Modocs.' I said. 'All I'm interested in is trying to restore peace.'

'I appreciate that, Riddle. If you sign up, I'll not force you into anything against your will.'

I pondered for a moment, then accepted.

A few days later, Wheaton held a conference in one of Van Bremer's barns. The atmosphere was pretty sober.

The officious Captain Bernard had arrived from Land's ranch. We sat round on bales of hay while Wheaton, looking weary, again went over the debacle.

'During the fight,' he said, 'the Modocs were never exposed to our fire. They fought from behind rocks. We had no targets to aim at. But I was proud of our soldiers.'

'Colonel,' Bernard cut in, 'the Klamaths were useless. They had no wish to fight. In fact I heard them conversing with the Modocs, shouting across the lines, and I believe they abandoned weapons and ammunition intentionally.'

Wheaton nodded. 'We shall send the Klamaths back to their reservation. We want Warm Springs Indians. They'll not let us down. We need at least a thousand foot soldiers, supported by howitzer fire, to get the Modocs out of their Stronghold. What's your opinion, Riddle?'

I said, 'Sending men across that ground south of the Stronghold is murderous. The more you send, the more are going to get killed.'

'What alternative is there?'

'Colonel,' I said. 'I'm here to make peace, not war. I'm not going to make suggestions which might cause more deaths, white or red.'

'I'm sorry, Riddle,' Wheaton said. 'I understand your attitude.'

Captain Bernard snorted impatiently. 'Riddle has associated with the Indians for many years. He can pass army plans onto Captain Jack any time he likes.'

Wheaton thumped the table. 'Captain Bernard, I will not have the integrity of Frank Riddle questioned. Nor will I have the wisdom of my decisions doubted.'

Bernard kept his mouth shut, but I

knew he wasn't satisfied.

Wheaton returned to his thoughts on the campaign. 'Maybe, we could attack from the lake, supported by gunboats firing cannon . . . ' He trailed off as an agitated orderly burst in.

'Beggin' your pardon, sir, but a supply train's been attacked by Modocs at Scorpion Point. Three men wounded, and the Injuns captured a whole lot of ammunition.'

Wheaton sighed, then said, 'That makes the situation even more urgent. We shall start building mortar-boats straight away. We must make plans to attack the Stronghold from the lake. We'll meet here again tomorrow.'

But twenty-four hours later when we re-assembled he had surprising news.

'I am pained to announce,' he said, 'that yesterday afternoon I received notification that I am to be relieved of this command. Colonel Alvan C. Gillem is to be your new commander. Gentlemen, I believe I am being used as a scapegoat.' His face was awash with bitterness. 'We must suspend building mortar-boats until Colonel Gillem arrives.'

As we dispersed, our mood was worsened by the weather. A blizzard was howling out of the north. Within days the entire territory was snow-bound. Supply trains couldn't reach us and our new commanding officer was stranded in San Francisco. But army scouts reported that Jack's Modocs appeared undaunted by the elements and ventured out from the Stronghold, moving around the Lava Beds, and beyond, as they pleased.

One freezing Thursday, I was summoned to Wheaton's tent. Apparently he had a visitor.

A Modoc woman was standing in front of Wheaton, guarded by several soldiers. I recognized her. She was Queen Mary, sister of Captain Jack. 'I am woman,' she said, giving me a nervous glance. 'Tell sojers not to point guns.'

I spoke to the guards and the rifles

were lowered. She had a strong, dark face and spoke in slow, positive words. 'Jack say him tired of fighting. He want Fairchild and you, Riddle, to come to Stronghold, talk things over.'

I translated her words. It was gratifying that Jack trusted me, but the thought of visiting the Stronghold was daunting.

'The new commander, Colonel Gillem,' Wheaton replied, 'must decide what is to be done. I will give him your message as soon as he arrives.'

I ensured that Queen Mary understood. Wheaton questioned her further.

'Some Modocs tired of fighting,' she said, 'but others not tired. Jack want peace. The children and old ones are cold — but he will have to do what the men vote in council. We have plenty of meat. Hooker Jim, Boston Charley and the others who killed settlers do not want peace because they'll be hanged. We have plenty cartridges and guns. Now I must go back before night comes.'

After she'd gone, I felt dejected. Things could drag on. I didn't fancy going into the Stronghold, even with John Fairchild as my companion. Some of the Indians would show little respect for a white flag.

Now everything was subject to the weather's whim. Thirty miles away at Louis Land's ranch, Bernard's command was quartered — and their morale was as low as ours. There had even been desertions.

It was three weeks before the thaw came. Colonel Gillem at last reported in, took command, and the disgruntled Wheaton departed.

Gillem was from Tennessee. He had a bullish face with a wide forehead and bushy beard. He was full of bluster. He decided on an immediate briefing for his officers and civilian scouts. When we were assembled, he strutted pompously up and down. 'President Grant is taking a personal interest in the Modoc trouble. I have drawn up new plans. Our camp will move from Van Bremer's to the base of Sheepy Ridge, so as to be close to the Modoc position. Other troops will take up positions on the eastern side of the Stronghold. But at present there will be no new onslaught against the Indians. A carefully selected team of peace negotiators, which includes Alfred Meacham, will shortly be arriving, and, along with them, will be General Canby, the Commander of the Department of Columbia. He's experienced in negotiating with Indians.'

Despite Gillem's tiresome manner, he was stating good news.

As he dismissed his officers, he beckoned me over. 'Mister Riddle,' he said. 'I want you and the rancher John Fairchild to go into the Modoc Stronghold and prepare the way for General Canby and the peace commissioners.'

I had been expecting this, but that didn't make the prospect any rosier.

7

A week later, we embarked on our risky mission. Needless to say, the brave John Fairchild had willingly agreed to accompany me to the Stronghold. He was a Southerner and he spoke in a slow drawl, and he had been one of the first ranchers to settle in the territory. He had always made a point of being friendly towards the Indians.

Gillem had moved our army camp from Van Bremer's to the base of Sheepy Ridge, which was now re-named 'Gillem's Bluff'. It was from here that General Canby and the peace commissioners intended to carry out their negotiations. They were expected to arrive soon.

The sun was shining as Fairchild and I walked out from the camp. I was carrying a large white cloth tied to a stick.

We moved along the shore of the lake, treading carefully so as not to twist our ankles on the treacherous rocks. The air was crisp and cold, yet I could feel sweat trickling down beneath my shirt. Even if we couldn't see a single Modoc, I guessed that our progress was being carefully watched.

We approached the solitary juniper tree that stood near the Stronghold. We were now treading the ground where the one-sided battle had been fought. Presently, we clambered over a chasm and the ground dipped down and ahead of us loomed the rocky ramparts of the Stronghold. Suddenly we spotted Scarfaced-Charley in his bright red bandanna, sitting on a chunk of rock. He was holding a rifle and wearing a weighty bandolier of ammunition, but he waved to us in a hospitable fashion.

Within minutes we had entered the Stronghold, and other Modoc warriors appeared, all heavily armed.

Scarfaced Charley led the way along a narrow trail. Fairchild and I followed and behind us came our welcoming party. We couldn't have turned tail now had we wanted to. The rocks that enclosed us were a jumble of large pockmarked cinders, piled into fortifications.

We passed behind rocky walls. No man could have fashioned a more perfect rifle gallery. Gazing from the cover of its embrasures, we could see right across the grim terrain.

'This place will be impossible to storm,' Fairchild whispered to me. 'The Modocs can shift their men around and direct their fire wherever it's needed.'

'And howitzer fire's not going to worry them with these caves to hide in,' I said.

After a moment we emerged in front of a gaping hole. This was Jack's cave and he was sitting on a rock at the entrance.

His face was creased with worry-lines. He was holding a rifle, but when he saw us he laid it aside and stood up and we all shook hands. 'I'm glad you come,' he said. 'Let's smoke a pipe.'

Other Modocs were appearing. Some of them were so weighed down with bandoliers they couldn't stand up straight. The area was pretty small, but soon they were hunkered down in a sort of semi-circle, three deep. I recognized many of them.

After we had smoked the pipe, Fairchild gave me words to translate. 'Jack, we understand you want to make peace.'

Jack nodded. 'We want no more war. If the whites let us live at Lost River — all of us — then there will be no more trouble.'

'You must tell General Canby this,' Fairchild said. 'The peace commission-ers will soon be ready to talk. But I think they will say you must stay on the reservation in the north.'

Jack sighed heavily. 'It's not good there. There's not enough to eat and the Klamaths hate us. Maybe we could stay here. This is not a good place, but it is better than the reservation. If we are to make the peace, why are the soldiers moving closer? They frighten my women and children. Will Canby make the soldiers go away?'

'Once a peace treaty has been made,' I explained.

'Then I will speak with this Canby,' Jack said.

'It will be best,' Fairchild said, 'to meet half-way between the soldier-camp and here.'

Jack nodded.

Hooker Jim suddenly spoke. 'If the peace is made, what will become of the Modocs who killed the settlers?'

Fairchild said, 'If these Modocs surrender, I expect they will be treated as prisoners of war, and they will not be put on trial for the killings.'

Hooker Jim gave a satisfied nod.

Jack turned to me. 'Go tell the commissioners that I am ready to hear them. Let your woman, Nan-ook-to-wa, come and tell me when Canby is ready to talk.'

I agreed.

I glanced and counted over twenty braves, armed like bandits, and there were more on guard-duty and hidden in the caves of the Stronghold. The atmosphere was suffocating. I imagined I could feel the heat of Modoc breath against my face. If the whim had taken them to kill us at that moment, it would have been done in a flash.

I was sure Jack would have given up long ago, had it not been for Hooker Jim and his killers seeking refuge with him in the Stronghold. As chief, he wouldn't betray them.

As we left the Stronghold, I wasn't confident. I believed that John Fairchild had given an assurance about Hooker Jim's future that Canby might not be able to honor. If that assurance was withdrawn, Jack would have no option but to fight to the death.

★　★　★

While we waited for the peace commissioners to come, lines of bivouacs were erected and reinforcements arrived — cavalry, infantry and artillery. Despite all the talk of peaceful negotiation, the military ring around the Modocs was tightening.

Ed Muybridge, a photographer from San Francisco, came to capture the scenes for posterity. He surprised me with a story that there were three Indian women from the Stronghold working the army tents as prostitutes. 'I tried to photograph them,' he said, 'but they wouldn't stand still. They slip in at night and soldiers pay them with ammunition. Sixty rounds is the going rate for a bed-partner.'

I shook my head in amazement. 'If peace negotiations break down, those soldier-boys will get shot with their own bullets!'

When Toby and I were out walking, we discovered a cave in the red volcanic rock, some two hundred yards north of the army camp. 'Let's make home here,' Toby suggested, 'and . . . '

'And what?' I didn't feel keen about moving.

'Tomorrow pay-day for sojers. They all get drunk. No good for us.'

I knew that drunkenness was such a problem that Gillem had issued an order: *No man is to have more than two drinks a day, and there is to be at least one hour's interval between drinks.* But this order was a joke because most of the noncoms were too drunk to make sure their men obeyed.

There was something else that influenced me. Professional gamblers were arriving on camp, and I'd struck a losing streak at Monte. Toby got real mean about me gambling away my wages, saying she'd withdraw her favors. So I decided I needed to avoid temptation.

That afternoon we moved home.

The cave was pretty shallow, but it provided some shelter, and from its mouth we could see out over Tule Lake. Toby was pleased with the stove I fashioned from an old chimney pipe, and we huddled around it. The wind was bitter-cold.

A few days later, some army officers climbed up through the rocks. Toby and I stepped outside to meet them. I recognized Colonel Gillem and the sandy-haired Reverend Eleazer Thomas clutching his bible. With them, was a tall, soldierly man.

'Mister Riddle,' Gillem announced, 'this is General Canby. He's come to take personal charge of events.'

The general gave my hand a warm shake, using both of his. There was something almost fatherly about his manner and his beardless face glowed with intense dedication. 'Mister Riddle, I understand that you have done brave work during this wretched affair, and I have come to personally thank you and your good lady.' He smiled in Toby's direction.

I said, 'Captain Jack has asked Toby to let him know when you are ready to hold a formal council with him.'

Canby nodded. 'We're waiting for

Leroy Dyar and Alfred Meacham to arrive. They've been delayed at the Klamath Reservation, and I will not start without them. But they should be here in a day or so.'

The Reverend Thomas said, 'We will pray that all parties will soon see wisdom.'

'We must be careful,' Colonel Gillem commented. 'The Modocs may try treachery.'

Canby waved his hand dismissively. 'I am used to dealing with Indians. They will soon appreciate I am here to make peace not war.'

'With all these soldiers surrounding them,' I said, 'Jack won't believe that.'

'I will invite the Modocs to visit the camp,' Canby said. 'They can see for themselves how futile war would be.'

Our visitors stayed for a half-hour. Eventually I could see that the general was anxious to leave and get on with his many tasks.

As he was going, he said, 'I'll let you know when Leroy Dyar and Alfred

Meacham arrive and the peace commissioners are ready to go to work. Your good lady can then carry word to Jack in the Stronghold.'

I said, 'Sure, General.'

That night, as we lay close to the warming fire in our cave, Toby said, 'Canby mustn't trust Modocs too much — especially not Hooker Jim and his father-in-law Curly Headed Doctor. I think they watch Jack to make sure he no give in to Canby.'

Two nights later we had some more visitors to our cave.

8

Toby had gone outside but shortly she rushed back. 'Frank, somebody coming!'

I unholstered my Navy Colt and took up position in the mouth of the cave. It was a dry night and the rocks were bathed with silvery moonlight. I saw movement down the slope, followed by the pant of heavy breathing — and then in Modoc a voice called out: 'It's Boston and Bogus. We come to warm ourselves by your fire.'

Toby was standing at my side. 'Don't hide in dark,' she called. 'Come into firelight so we see you.'

Like shadowy spirits, they crept in. Not until they were seated by our fire, gulping down coffee, did I put my gun aside. They both had killed white people, despite the fact that they looked scarcely more than boys.

They'd come from the Stronghold, crossing the lake by canoe, making sure the soldiers didn't spot them.

The pale-skinned Boston Charley was heavy-shouldered, with a cunning expression. He was wearing a tattered brown coat and an old cap. Bogus was much taller and had a blanket thrown about his shoulders. He spoke some English and was constantly grinning.

'We stay here tonight,' he stated. 'Tomorrow we go see sojer-camp, like Canby say.'

I nodded. This was the craziest war I'd ever known, with the two sides paying visits, sometimes chatting like friends, and at other times murdering each other.

Our two guests boasted that despite the army presence the Modocs were roaming as they pleased through the lava country, easily avoiding the soldiers, and rustling all the cattle they needed.

Toby talked with our visitors, while I watched them, seeing how their eyes darted about, studying the surroundings. But it seemed they did not plan our immediate murder because they talked excitedly of me conducting them around the army camp in the morning. I knew that Canby would show friendship, but I hoped he would understand that these visitors were nothing better than spies.

That night I stayed alert, listening to the snores of the Modocs, my pistol within reach. Next morning, Toby went to inform Canby that the Indians were accepting his invitation for a visit. A half-hour later, I took them through the army lines and the general appeared in person, shaking their hands, giving them cigars. He drew me aside, whispering, 'Show them as many soldiers and guns as possible. Scare them if you can, then maybe they'll go back to Jack and convince him to surrender.'

I nodded and accompanied the Indians as they roamed freely through the camp. They watched soldiers packing hollow mortar shells with gun-powder, rock chippings and rifle balls.

'Cannon balls are same size as men's heads,' Bogus grinned. 'It's like throwing men's heads at each other!' For a moment they were almost helpless with laughter. When Boston Charley turned to me, there were tears of mirth glistening on his pale cheeks.

'Exploding heads no good against Modocs,' he boasted. 'Bluebellies'll never drive Jack out of Stronghold.'

Presently, they saw boats ferrying supplies and messages to the command at the eastern end of the lake, nine miles away. After that, we climbed to Signal Rock, a third of the way up the bluff, and signalers put on a special demonstration with their big flags.

Boston Charley shook his head in disgust. 'It not fair for sojers to talk with flags.'

The tour continued and the Modocs made exclamations of surprise at the array of weapons and manpower.

Presently, the two Indians returned with me to our cave, carrying a sack of supplies that Canby had given them. He had also given them a message for Jack. 'If he surrenders, we will discuss a future home for the Modocs.'

When Boston and Bogus finally departed, both Toby and I sighed with relief.

★　★　★

Canby ordered soldiers to erect a small tent in no-man's land, half way between the army camp and the Modoc stronghold. Here, future pow-wows could be held and could be observed from Signal Rock.

Two mornings later, I awoke to discover that Toby was not in the cave. I walked over to the army camp and found Alfred Meacham unpacking his bags. 'Good to see you, Frank,' he said. 'Leroy Dyar and I got in yesterday. Now we're all here, the peace commission can get to work.'

'Have you seen Toby?' I enquired.

'Yes. Canby wants to arrange a meeting at the peace tent at noon next Friday. He sent Toby to the Stronghold to inform Jack.'

I nodded. I felt worried about Toby. I knew there were some Modocs who mistrusted her, believing that she was betraying her people.

Meacham kept talking. 'Knowing that I understand the Modocs well, the President asked me to act as chairman of the present peace commission. One day, Mister Riddle, I intend to write a book about the Modocs and present their side of the dispute.'

'I hope it has a happy ending,' I said.

Presently I returned to our cave, spent a long hour waiting and then was greatly relieved to see Toby clambering up the rocks, having left her mare at the army camp. She was agitated, and I led her into the cave, made her sit down.

'Frank,' she at last gasped. 'I give Canby's message to Jack. He agree to meet Canby at the tent on Friday. But most Modocs are in bad mood. They want another big fight. They don't trust the whites.' She paused, biting her lip in distress. She went on. 'As I leave Stronghold, a cousin called Weium block my path. He look round, make sure nobody watching, then he say Modocs plan to kill commissioners when they come for pow-wow. Hooker Jim and rest of them talk Jack into agreeing. Jack is to kill Canby, Hooker Jim kill Meacham and . . . '

'That's crazy,' I gasped. 'Surely they know treachery will bring the whole army down on them.'

I remembered Weium. He was a young warrior with a heart-shaped face, and I knew him to be honest.

Toby went on. 'They believe if they kill Canby and peace commissioners, all sojers go away.'

I thought for a moment, then said, 'I've got to warn Canby.'

She nodded, her tawny eyes moist with concern. I hugged her close. It seemed her moods reflected the sorrows of the entire world — and thankfully its joys as well.

I ran all the way to the army camp, going straight to Canby's tent. The sentry didn't want to allow me in, saying the general was in conference, but I brushed him aside and entered. Canby was seated at a table with Colonel Gillem, Alfred Meacham, the Reverend Thomas and Leroy Dyar. Their faces registered disapproval at my intrusion, but I got straight to the point. 'General, my woman has just returned from the Stronghold. She gave your message to Jack, but she learned something else. Before I tell you, you must promise to keep it to yourself. If word leaks out, Toby's life will be in real danger. So will mine.'

Canby lit his cigar. 'Whatever you say will be treated in confidence.'

I looked at Eleazer Thomas. He said, 'I am a minister of the gospel. I have my God to meet and I promise I'll never divulge any secret.'

The others were nodding.

So I explained what Toby had learned. 'I tell you the truth. They intend to kill you at the pow-wow.'

Canby briefly pondered, then said, 'Mister Riddle, why should they do that? There are only a few of them against hundreds of us.'

'If these Indians have decided to kill you,' I said. 'all Heaven's angels won't stop them!'

'I'm sure Frank is right.' Dyar said.

'I agree with Frank,' Alfred Meacham said, removing his pipe from his mouth. 'You must remember that the Indians have suffered treachery and will have no hesitation at dealing it out.'

'Alfred,' Canby said, 'it's very easy for rumors to spread.' For a moment he sat deep in thought. At last he turned to me. 'I think you're exaggerating the danger, Mister Riddle. I can't believe the Indians would be so foolhardy as to try to kill us in full view of nearly a thousand soldiers.'

'Your men will be a mile-and-a-half away,' I argued. 'By the time they reach the tent, it'll be too late.'

'I respect your opinion,' Canby said, 'but I am determined to go to the council tent on Friday and show good faith.'

I was furious at his complacency. 'General, if you go to the council tent the Modocs will kill you!'

'Mr Riddle,' Canby said, 'I am a military man and I have to go where my duty calls. But if you and your wife are so convinced that there is danger, then it would be quite wrong of me to ask you to interpret for us at the pow-wow. I'll understand if you wish to withdraw.'

'You'd have nobody to translate,' I said.

'Boston Charley would do it,' Canby commented.

'A snake would make a more honest job of it!' I retorted. 'We'll come. We'll do our best to talk them out of murder, but I fear the worst.'

Canby nodded. The discussion was finished.

I knew that the real, terrible moment of truth would come at the peace tent on Friday. Nothing would turn Canby back now.

9

Toby and I knew murder was afoot. Maybe in his heart, Canby knew too, but he wasn't going to admit it. He believed that the principles at stake were more important than all else — even his own and other people's lives.

All too soon, the morning of Good Friday, April 11, 1873 arrived. The sky was cloudless blue. All the snow had disappeared and the rocky hillsides were bright with purple larkspur, orange poppies and white lavender.

Toby and I walked to the peace commissioners' tents.

Reverend Thomas, dressed in a gray tweed suit, was giving Leroy Dyar a sermon: 'The Good Lord has decreed that today will see the end of the war.'

Boston Charley, who seemed to be making Gillem's Camp his second home, was sitting next to Thomas, sharing coffee from the reverend's cup. After a while, Thomas went into his tent and returned with a set of clothing, which he gave to the Indian. 'A gesture of good will,' he said.

Meanwhile, Bogus was talking to Meacham, trying to persuade him to wear some smart new boots.

'Old shoes will be better for walking over the rocks,' Meacham said. 'Why do you want me to wear the new boots?'

'They look better,' Bogus grinned.

At that moment I was even more sure that Bogus intended that Meacham would die and he wanted those boots for himself.

General Canby appeared, looking immaculate in his full-dress uniform with its buttons, braid and medals. 'I know Jack appreciates military uniforms,' he said. 'We must put on a show for him.' He turned to the two Indians. 'Go back to Jack. Tell him that the commissioners will be at the tent. We're ready to talk.'

The Modocs scurried away.

Meacham came up to me and produced a small derringer pistol. 'Doctor Cabbaniss gave me this,' he said. 'I don't know whether I should take it or not.'

'I think you should,' I said.

He hesitated, then nodded and slipped it into his vest pocket.

General Canby came striding up. 'Gentlemen' he said, 'I know we are at risk, but the importance of our objective justifies that risk. The Indians have promised to be unarmed. I've given orders that we should be kept under constant surveillance from Signal Rock. If we are molested our men will immediately come to our help. We've agreed to speak with the Indians and we must keep our word.'

Thomas piped in: 'I have prayed that the Good Lord will smile upon us. We are in his hands.'

At that moment we saw Boston and Bogus returning, hurrying up through the picket lines. Soon they told us that

Jack was already at the peace-tent, awaiting our arrival.

It seemed hopeless. Dyar and Meacham knew that we were embarking on a suicidal mission, but they were too proud to back out. Toby was going because she felt she might be able to stave off the murder. I was going because I was plumb crazy.

General Canby issued some final instructions to his orderly and his secretary, then he went into his tent and emerged carrying a box of Havanas. 'I haven't got a peace-pipe,' he smiled. 'We'll have to smoke cigars instead.'

Marching with his head held high, he strode out through the picket-lines, following the foot trail. Reverend Thomas followed at his heels, his lips moving as he prayed. Alongside him was Boston Charley mounted on a horse, a rifle tucked under his arm. At least one Modoc, despite the previously agreed conditions, was armed.

Meacham, his teeth grinding on his pipe-stem, and Dyar, and Toby perched on her sidesaddle, were all riding horses, but I preferred to walk beside them. If bullets started to fly out there, a horse would be a handicap.

It was a mile-and-a-half from the army camp to the peace tent. Our little cavalcade moved along the lake shore. I glanced over my shoulder and saw Bogus bringing up the rear. He too was looking back, no doubt to make sure no soldiers were following.

'Let's hope the look-outs on Signal Rock are not drunk today,' Meacham whispered to me. 'If there's any monkey business at the tent, they better raise the alarm quickly.'

Dyar had overheard him. 'They're too far away to help us,' he said.

I noticed we were one short. 'Where's Colonel Gillem?' I asked.

'Sick in his tent,' Meacham explained.

'I don't blame him,' Dyar said.

At this time, Bogus and Boston surged ahead to let Jack know we were coming.

Suddenly a quick scuttle in the rocks made me jump, then I relaxed. It was only a kangaroo-rat hopping madly away from our intrusion. Otherwise everywhere was unnaturally still, the only sound being the scrape of our feet and the blowing of the horses.

The tent came into view. Standing near it were eight Indians, including Boston and Bogus who were openly holding rifles. The original agreement had been for five unarmed Modocs — but I suspected Canby would not complain.

As we approached, the Indians came forward to greet us. Jack was wearing a threadbare coat and an old slouch hat. He looked anxious. He didn't bother to play-act like the rest of them, with their grinning, hearty welcomes. To Jack's right was Ellen's Man, cherubic-faced and soft-looking, but his appearance could hoodwink you. He had a reputation for viciousness. John Schonchin stood at Jack's left, his scrawny throat encircled by a bear-claw choker, and

102

behind him were Shacknasty Jim, so called because of untidy habits, and Black Jim, Jack's dusky half-brother. The muscular Hooker Jim hovered close by.

The day was dry, so there was no question of talking in the tent. Instead Jack led the way to a sagebrush fire on the east side. I noticed with unease how the bulk of the tent would hide us from the view of the soldiers on Signal Rock. Proceedings would be further masked by the sagebrush smoke.

If Canby had similar worries, he didn't show them. He smilingly shook hands with each of the Indians. I noticed how John Schonchin's coat sagged open, revealing a revolver tucked into his belt. No doubt the others were also armed.

After he passed round the cigars and we had lit up with brands from the fire, Canby seated himself on a round boulder, facing Jack. Meacham had dismounted from his horse. He took off his coat, draped it over his saddle-horn.

He sat on the ground near to John Schonchin and Thomas joined them. Toby slid from her horse, and we squatted near to Canby, ready to do our interpreting. Dyar remained standing beside his horse, no doubt poised to react if things turned ugly.

As Chairman of the Commissioners, Meacham opened the proceedings, speaking slowly. 'Toby, tell Jack that General Canby wants to ensure the Modocs get a fair deal.'

Toby carefully translated Meacham's words.

Jack replied, 'There has been too much fighting. Our children are always crying. If the soldiers are sent home we can make peace. We can't make peace while they surround us.'

Meacham took a draw in his cigar. 'The soldiers are here for your protection. If your people come out of the Stronghold, we can offer you a better place to live.'

I could see Hooker Jim pacing restlessly behind Jack's back. My eyes suddenly met his, but he glanced away. He looked towards the army camp, then he walked over to Meacham's sorrel. To make escape easier, Meacham had left the animal untethered, but Hooker Jim fastened the reins to the sagebrush. He picked up the coat, which Meacham had draped across the saddle, and pulled it on. All at once he seemed to notice that the talking had stopped and he was the focus of attention. He assumed an air of bravado, swaggering towards us. 'Me old man Meacham now,' he grinned. 'You no think me like old man Meacham, eh?'

Meacham forced a laugh, treating it as a joke. He removed his hat and said, 'Hooker Jim, you'd better take my hat too!'

Hooker Jim's grin widened. 'There's no hurry, old man,' he said. 'I will have the hat soon.'

The words were ominous. Toby didn't translate, but everybody got the message anyway.

Canby tried to calm the situation. 'Jack, you must trust me. I have always been a good friend to the Indians.'

After Toby had translated, the Reverend Thomas started on one of his sermons, pausing to allow Toby to translate. He advised the Indians to give up the old religious beliefs and take the white man's god. He finished by saying that General Canby was an honorable and God-fearing man.

He made little impression on Jack. John Schonchin said, 'If the white man will give us Willow Creek Valley and take the soldiers away, then there will be no more trouble.'

The atmosphere was tight as a drum. Every word, movement and gesture seemed forced, like make-believe actions in a stage play. Jack looked tense, engrossed in some inner turmoil.

Dyar, sensing impending violence, walked behind his horse. I stood up and pretended to adjust the stirrup of Toby's animal. Toby had pressed herself down on the ground. She yawned and made out she was tired. I knew her heart, like mine, was thumping. Suddenly Jack issued an ultimatum: 'Take the soldiers away, then we'll talk about leaving the Stronghold.'

Canby shook his head.

Hopelessness settled over the Modoc chief's face. There was no way back for him. He looked Canby straight in the eye. In a rock-hard voice he repeated his ultimatum.

Canby again shook his head. 'Jack, not yet.'

Wildness blazed from the chief's eyes. He shouted, 'You've had your chance, Canby! Let us do it!'

He pulled a revolver from under his coat and Toby screamed, 'No, Jack!'

As Jack raised his gun, there was a scurrying movement from the direction of the Stronghold. Out of the bushes burst two more Modocs, Slolux and Barncho, brandishing rifles.

At that moment Jack pulled his trigger; the gun made a thunderous 'click' as it misfired.

Canby could have run, but he remained still, a look of disbelief on his face as Jack re-cocked his gun and raised it again.

Jack fired point blank into Canby's face, jerking him backwards over the boulder in a splattering of gore. Everybody was shouting. The Modocs had snatched pistols from their coats and the air was suddenly alive with bullets.

Instinct had me throwing myself to the side, rolling beneath the rearing legs of Toby's horse. From my prone position, I glimpsed Boston Charley standing over Reverend Thomas, firing his rifle into the helpless cleric. Meanwhile, amazingly, Canby had staggered to his feet, was lurching blindly towards the army camp — but he tripped and fell. Ellen's Man shot him as he lay on the ground, making his body jerk like a rag doll. Next, Jack, brandishing a knife, knelt beside Canby. He plunged his fingers into the general's hair, yanking his head back.

Then, as if he was slaughtering a cow, he slashed the general's throat, nigh cutting his head off.

There was a lot of scrambling and guns blasting off, then Ellen's Man turned, peering at me through the smoke. He raised his rifle. I ran, stumbling over the rocks as he fired. The whine of lead scorched the air, but his aim was poor. Fear drove every thought but escape from my brain. Up ahead I glimpsed Dyar running. Hooker Jim was after him, but Dyar twisted round and fired a derringer at the Indian, missing but scaring him away.

For a moment I was convinced the whole pack would come after me. I ran maybe twenty paces before I looked back. I was clear of the immediate struggle. I was desperate for sight of Toby. I grunted in dismay. I could see Meacham sprawled on the ground. Shacknasty Jim was pulling the clothes from his body. Slolux placed a rifle at Meacham's head, but Shacknasty pushed him away, crying out: 'Don't spoil clothes!'

Like a wolf greedy for more carrion, Boston left Thomas's body and joined the group around Meacham. I stood transfixed, helpless to do anything. I saw Boston draw a knife, place his foot on Meacham's neck and start to scalp him, ripping off a side lock of hair — but at that moment Toby appeared, hurling herself onto Boston, trying to drag him clear. Boston turned angrily, cuffed her away, knocking her down, then he swung back to Meacham, anxious to complete the scalping. But Toby wasn't finished. Scrambling up, she glanced in the direction of the army camp. She clapped her hands to attract attention and her shrill words carried clearly, '*Sojers coming!*'

I saw Jack, shouting and gesturing for his men to fall back.

I gazed towards Gillem's Bluff. I could see no soldiers. The only movement came from Dyar's fast-retreating figure.

I realized the Modocs were heeding

Toby's warning. Boston had given up trying to scalp Meacham. He gave the body a final, spiteful kick, then ran after the other Modocs back towards the Stronghold. Some of them were carrying the bloodstained clothing they'd torn from the bodies. I saw Jack speak briefly to Toby, then he took to his heels. Toby had been stooping over Meacham's body. She straightened up and saw me.

'Meacham no dead!' she shouted. 'Get doctor quick!'

I hesitated.

'Go goddam quick!' she screamed.

So I left her and started for the army camp, running along the lake shore.

Afterwards, a lot of folks branded me a coward for leaving my wife right then, but I was certain she was safe. The Modocs had fled. Meacham, if he still survived, needed medical help.

Toby had affected a good ruse in screaming that soldiers were coming. But they weren't. I was almost back to Gillem's Bluff, catching up with the flagging Dyar, when we met the newspaper reporters, Fox and Atwell.

Dyar panted out: 'All dead — except us!' which he believed to be true.

'Where are the Indians now?' Atwell asked.

'Gone back to Stronghold!'

With note pads ready, the two reporters rushed on, anxious to reach the scene of the massacre.

I was winded. I slumped to the ground, dazed and sick. I cursed Gillem for his slowness in dispatching a relief force, cursed Canby for his rashness, cursed the Modocs for their insane butchery.

As an army bugle sounded, I remembered Toby and Meacham. I glanced up and saw a skirmish-line of troopers approaching. Soon, a sergeant was helping me to my feet. 'They need a doctor out there mighty bad!' I gasped.

He nodded and sent a runner to camp for a doctor.

My boots were split by the rocks,

reddened by the blood seeping from my feet, but, finding my second wind, I joined the soldiers, rushing back towards the peace tent, desperate to find my wife, and sick at the prospect of the carnage that awaited us.

10

For a while I stayed behind the skirmish line as the soldiers moved across the uneven ground, but soon impatience grew in me and I started to overtake them. As I did so, I caught up with the sergeant.

'Why,' I panted . . . 'were you so goddamned long coming?'

He kept glancing round, wary in case Modocs leaped from the rocks. I glanced over my shoulder. I could see more soldiers coming out from camp, following us.

'We all formed up, ready to move,' the sergeant responded, 'but there was some sort of confusion over the order.'

He turned, shouting at his men to hurry, then he swung back to me. 'The general, Meacham, Thomas,' he huffed, ' . . . all dead?'

'Maybe Meacham's still alive . . . but only just.'

'Jesus Christ! What a mess.'

When we reached the peace tent, the two reporters were already there. I saw Meacham sprawled on the ground. Toby was leaning over him — and Atwell was busy writing on his pad.

Poor Meacham was in no condition to be interviewed, but amazingly he moved, forcing himself into a sitting position, then he staggered to his feet. He started to howl — a despairing, agonized sound. He was naked, except for his flannel drawers. Every inch of him was glistening with blood. Half his scalp had been sliced from his skull and was hanging across his face. He pushed aside Toby's helping hands and stumbled forward. He was crazy with pain, blinded by blood, unaware of what was happening.

In that instant a soldier alongside me noticed him and cried out, 'There's a damned Injun!' He was raising his rifle.

'No, you fool!' I yelled and knocked

the weapon aside.

No bullet had been fired, but Meacham dropped like a stone, and Toby and I reached him and fell to our knees. He was still breathing, even conscious, but he had been shot many times. Half his ear had been hacked off. His breath came in faltering gasps.

'He won't last long,' I told Toby.

She ripped away part of her skirt and started to wipe the blood from his face.

'Before Jack run off,' she told me, 'he say he sorry for what happen. He say his men make him do it.'

'Too late to be sorry,' I said.

I came to my feet as more soldiers rushed up. 'Canby's over there!' I pointed to the south of the tent, and shortly we found the general. He was lying on his back, quite dead. He was completely naked, and his throat had been so deeply slashed that his scalped head rested against his shoulder. Three bullet wounds showed on his pale body.

I scrambled to where the Reverend Thomas lay. He too was naked. With gentle hands, soldiers had turned his body over. His head was a gory mess of spilled brains. Beneath his body a corporal found a purse and for some reason counted the contents. 'Sixty dollars,' he said. He returned the money to the purse, closed it and placed it respectfully in the clergyman's lifeless hands.

By now stretcher parties had arrived. Ed Muybridge, the photographer, was busy taking pictures. Doctor Cabbaniss was pressing a bottle to Meacham's lips but he struggled against it, his words scarcely audible. 'I . . . can't drink brandy. I'm a . . . temperance man!'

Ten minutes later I saw him sitting up on a stretcher giving the persistent Atwell a groaning, halting account of the awful events of the day. But before long he had slumped down onto his stretcher. Somebody murmured, 'He's gone!' and covered his head with a blanket, but Toby drew it back.

At that moment I noticed a corporal stooping over Canby's corpse. He was poking a finger in his mouth. He extracted the general's false teeth and slipped them into his pocket, maybe thinking they might be worth good money one day.

Now, the order was given to withdraw.

Hardly a man spoke as our column moved slowly back to camp, bearing the mutilated bodies. The light was fading, snow was falling and the wind howled a mournful tune.

When we approached the camp, men rushed out to meet us. Gillem, looking pale, stood tugging at his beard, for once speechless. He watched as the bodies were carried past him. We had no time to pause.

Cabbaniss instructed us to carry Meacham to the field hospital. Another doctor, Semig, and several orderlies joined Cabbaniss and they quickly got to work. Almost forgotten, Toby and I stood in the tent's shadows and watched as Meacham was lifted onto the operating table.

118

Orderlies held lanterns and the doctors made their initial examination, their words carrying clearly to us.

'Guess somebody fired point-blank into his face . . . but the bullet must've bounced off his thick skull.'

'Even if he does survive, he'll most likely be blind. I'll get his scalp and ear stitched up first.'

Cabbaniss took a needle and thread from the lapel of his coat while orderlies sponged away blood. Meacham had bullet wounds in his shoulder, chest, arms and hand. Cabbaniss replaced the flap of scalp in its rightful position, then he started to sew. Meanwhile, Semig got to work, probing out embedded lead. Toby now lent a hand, fetching and carrying bowls. Meacham started to groan, but a swab of chloroform quieted him.

Toby suddenly turned to me. 'Frank.' she said. 'Your feet are all cut and bleeding. You go heat water, soak them in bowl.'

I nodded and left them dressing

Meacham's wounds.

An hour later, having done as I was told and put on different boots, I noticed a hammering sound coming from the carpenters' compound. There, I discovered two gun-cases had been fashioned into coffins, obviously for Canby and Thomas. A third casket was almost completed and the carpenter was standing back to admire his work.

'Meacham's still alive,' I said. 'That third coffin may not be needed.'

The carpenter gave me a despairing look. 'I hope I ain't been wasting my time,' he said.

That evening, while Toby nursed Meacham, I drew a tent from the quartermaster and pitched it close to the field hospital.

At 3 P.M. flag signals were received from Hospital Rock. Donald McKay and his Indians had arrived there. They were replacements for the disgraced Klamath scouts. The lanky McKay was half-Scot and half-Indian. I had never trusted him. He'd drunk me under the table more than once. The scouts he commanded were Indians from the Warm Springs reservation. They all shared a long-standing hatred of the Modocs.

11

Monday morning found us gathered in the large tent used for conferences.

'Gentlemen,' Gillem said, 'I've received orders from General Sherman. We are to attack the Modocs and be fully justified in their utter extermination.'

An exclamation of approval whipped through the assembled officers. All were hungry for action.

'Our general's wicked murder will spark off a surge of restlessness through the western tribes,' Gillem continued. 'Fort Klamath has been placed on full alert. The enemy must be annihilated. We have seven hundred fifty men. They have maybe seventy warriors in the Stronghold. Our attack will be launched tonight. Every man will be issued with one hundred rounds of ammunition. Major Mason will move from the east, supported by howitzer fire. Major

Green will have overall command in the western flank. Troops F and K will advance from the west. Should any Indians leave the Stronghold to attack, then the cavalry is to charge and cut them off. All men will fight dismounted. During the night, the Stronghold will be bombarded with mortar fire, forcing the Indians to take cover in their caves. The two prongs of our attack must link up between the lake and the Stronghold, thus depriving the Indians of their water supply. Our enemy will then have no alternative but to submit. Victory will be ours.'

He paused as a cheer surged through his listeners, then he said, 'And there is one other message I have for you. President Grant has appointed Colonel Jefferson C. Davis to succeed General Canby but he will not be here for a week or so yet. By the time he arrives I am determined that we will have successfully concluded the campaign.'

'Davis!' I heard Major Mason exclaim to Green. 'A few years back he got court-martialled on murder charges!'

'Well,' Green remarked, 'maybe he'll have a few Modocs to murder now.'

When the conference broke up, officers hurried away. The quartermaster was soon issuing every man with equipment. A renewed sense of purpose and lust for revenge had the camp bustling with activity.

I walked to the hospital tent where Toby was sitting with the heavily bandaged Meacham. 'How is he?' I enquired. She looked weary but I knew she would not rest while there was work to do.

'If his wounds don't go bad,' she said, 'he live.'

Meacham actually grinned at me. 'I'm a tough old coot,' he whispered.

'Can you see all right now?' I asked.

'Sure I can. I need my eyes to be able to write my book. In the book I'll not justify what Jack did. But I want to explain the Modoc side of this business. All right is not on the side of the whites.'

I was amazed. After all he'd suffered at the hands of the Indians, he still sympathized with them. 'The sad thing,' he went on, 'is that the only solution to this present conflict is the crushing of the Modoc Nation by military force.'

I nodded. He was growing tired.

★ ★ ★

There was no moon. By starlight we watched the army columns form up. It was 2 A.M. and all men had been cautioned to keep as quiet as possible. Orders were whispered and men moved carefully over the rocks. I returned to my tent, tried to get some sleep but could not.

Meanwhile, I knew that the troops would be moving into their pre-planned positions, both on this side of the Stronghold and in the east, where Major Mason's column was supported by Donald McKay's Warm Spring Indians.

'Maybe Gillem make same mistakes Wheaton made.' Toby commented.

I shook my head. 'For one thing, the artillery won't be hampered by fog — and secondly, Gillem'll be able to keep in touch with the troops in the east. He's using boats on the lake to ferry men and supplies to Hospital Rock and Scorpion Point.'

At 6 A.M. the howitzers on Hospital Rock started lobbing exploding shells into the Stronghold, but soon, across the intervening ground, we could hear the Modocs howling defiance. Their voices echoed around the rocks, making it seem they were in their thousands.

Just after dawn, the first casualty arrived at the field hospital. A young private was stretchered in, waving his arms in anguish. With Toby, I hurried to the hospital tent to find Doctor Semig examining him. He straightened up, shaking his head. 'A severe dose of alcoholism,' he said. 'When he sobers up, he can go back to the battle.'

As daylight came, the crack of rifle

shots grew fiercer. It was easy to tell the difference between the 'ping' of the Modocs' Henry repeaters and the loud bang of the army's new guns. Toby and I climbed to Chimney Rock, next to Signal Point, for a clearer view of the battle. Across the Lava Beds, puffs of gun smoke indicated the positions of the soldiers. We could see how a line of men would rush forward under the covering fire of their comrades, then take refuge behind boulders and provide similar cover as the line overlapped them and advanced a few more yards.

Major Green's west-side force had gained their intended position. On the eastern flank, soldiers made a successful charge and gained a rocky hillock. On their right, a desperate skirmish raged as an attempt was made to join Green's force to Mason's. This was thwarted by hot Modoc fire.

We could see how Indian snipers were not confined to the Stronghold. They lay hidden in the rocks, falling back as the soldiers advanced. In places the army was forced to retreat, but gradually ground was taken and held.

Throughout the day, casualties were brought back to the hospital-tent. The first was Captain Perry's sixteen-year-old trumpeter who was shot through the head. He survived for several hours, constantly crying out in agony. When he eventually died, it was a relief to all.

I worked with Toby, comforting the wounded, giving them sips of water, fetching and carrying for the doctors. Men were stretchered in with shattered thighbones, shrapnel injuries, broken limbs, sprained ankles or lacerated hands and knees. A man, his pelvis broken, died on the operating table.

That night, when darkness settled over the Lava Beds, the advance was halted and positions were consolidated. I carried Doctor Cabbaniss's bag as he toured the battlefield and treated the wounded. He was determined not to leave the injured where the Modocs could capture them.

Men had piled up rock shelters and

sat eating their rations. Meanwhile, the air reverberated with the thump of mortar fire as shells were directed into the Stronghold.

Next day, April 16, followed much the same pattern, with soldiers moving closer to the Stronghold, though with some cost. At the hospital tent, surgeons worked tirelessly, sometimes saving a patient, sometimes not. Frequently a man would be given a slug of whiskey and a bullet to bite on, and then held down struggling as an amputation saw was brought to bear. Men cried out in shuddering anguish and there wasn't enough chloroform to relieve them.

During the afternoon, news came that Green's and Mason's columns had linked together north of the Stronghold and were holding the ground, cutting the Modocs off from their water supply.

Next day, just after dawn, Gillem sent for me. He had returned from an inspection of the battlefield and was pleased with the progress made. 'Perhaps by tomorrow, Mister Riddle, we will have taken the Stronghold.'

He'd produced a satchel. 'I'll appreciate if you'll travel by boat and deliver these orders to Major Mason at Hospital Rock. Their delivery is extremely important.'

'I'll hand them to him personally,' I said. I took the satchel and left him, walking down to the lake where several small white-hulled boats were moored. I was expected.

Soon, we had pushed off. I sat in the stern as the boat's three-man crew worked at their oars. We moved far out onto the lake, making sure we were beyond range of any snipers. Meanwhile the rattle of fire sounded clearly as the battle in the Lava Beds continued.

Today the lake was calm, the sun bright. It took us a half-hour to reach Hospital Point, which was an outcropping jutting into the lake. To the south, its low parapets gave some cover, if a man kept his head down. Being at a slight elevation it commanded a good view of the Stronghold and the intervening terrain. It had gained its name because during Wheaton's ill-fated January campaign the wounded had been treated here. Now, with most of the men involved in the advance towards the Stronghold, there were only a few soldiers present. I asked for Major Mason and was informed that he had gone forward to inspect his troops. I decided to go and look for him, climbed over the parapet and struck out over the spiteful ground.

I passed the point where the Coehorn Mortars were set up. At this moment they had curtailed their bombardment for fear of hitting their own men who were quite close to the Stronghold. I again enquired for the major, shouting above the noise of rifle fire, and an artilleryman waved me forward.

I'd gone about twenty yards when I heard a groaning sound. Glancing around, I discovered a man lying in a rocky crevice. He had his hands over his face. By means of introduction I said, 'You hurt?'

An impatient eye peeped out from between his fingers and he gasped, 'Am I hurt? What a damn-fool question to ask. Is a man hurt when he has all his insides shot out and scattered about on the ground?'

I searched around. 'Can't see no innards,' I said.

I had a closer look at him. His shirt sleeve showed a little blood above the elbow. A bullet had grazed him and, being near spent, had wedged itself in a pair of buckskin gloves tucked in his blouse on the right side.

'You've persuaded yourself you're bad-hit,' I said. I took the lead in my hand and gave it to him. 'Keep it as a lucky souvenir.'

He gazed at the bullet with amazed eyes. 'Well I'll be dawgone,' he said.

Minutes later, I found Major Mason, standing on a rock, gazing in the direction of the Stronghold. A few yards to his front, his men were taking shelter in stoneworks originally thrown up by the Modocs.

He nodded a greeting, and read carefully through the dispatch Gillem had sent him. 'We are to storm the Stronghold by three o'clock this afternoon,' he said. He turned again towards the Stronghold and then cursed. 'Seems we might have taken it before then. Look at those fools!'

My gaze followed his pointing arm. On the Stronghold rocks, no more than one hundred fifty yards from where we stood, the Indians had displayed a white animal skin dangling from a pole. It was their sacred flag.

'All along,' Mason was saying, 'my boys have been swearing they wanted to take that damned flag before Gillem's men reached it.'

One of his sergeants was crawling up across the rocks towards the flag. He reached a point where, by stretching out, he could grasp the pole. With a final flourish he pulled it down, no doubt expecting a hail of bullets — but none came. In a surge of bravado, he jumped up and, in full view of the encircling troops, waved the flag above his head. His shouted challenge to the Modocs was heard by everybody:

'Come out of your holes, you red bastards!'

For a moment there was a stunned silence. No Indian rose to the bait. Then, all around, soldiers were moving out from behind their cover. No orders had been given, but all at once there was an undisciplined charge into the Stronghold. At any moment we expected to be met by bullets. I ran alongside Mason, stumbling across craggy rocks. The army had waited six months for this moment. Nothing would stop them now.

I entered the Stronghold. Still there were no Indian war whoops or shots. Soldiers stampeded along the labyrinth of paths, looking into the caves, climbing onto the battlements. Isolated shots rang out, screams. As I came round a shoulder of rock, I stumbled over a crouched soldier. He was scalping the lifeless body of an old Modoc man. I tried to pull him off, but he pushed me back, waving his bloody knife in my face. 'This is my business, squaw man!' he snarled. 'An hour ago, I found the bones of my best friend in the Lava Beds, butchered by Modoc devils last January. They'd chopped his fingers off. Don't you try to stop me!'

I didn't argue. I stumbled past him, and coming round a bluff, I saw a group of soldiers. An officer was with them. They were holding an old Modoc woman prisoner. I ran past them. A moment later I heard the snap of a pistol-shot. I glanced back. Surely they hadn't killed the woman! The rocks obscured my view. I hesitated, then ran on.

Right now, a startling fact dawned on me. Apart from a few old men and women, the Stronghold was deserted. Jack and his people had vanished!

12

I reached Jack's cave. For a moment I stood near the natural rostrum overlooking the entrance. This was where Fairchild and I had talked to Jack and trembled for our lives. This must also have been where plans had been made to kill the Peace Commissioners. Now only the ghosts of memories remained.

I glanced about. Everywhere, rocks were scarred where mortar shells had exploded, but deep in their caves, the Indians would have been safe.

'Where in God's name have they all gone?' one soldier kept asking. 'Can't just disappear off the face of the earth!'

I walked on, passing more deserted pits and caves. Soldiers were swarming through the Stronghold, hunting for souvenirs, but little of value had been left.

I moved along narrow pathways, the

rocks almost brushing my shoulders on both sides. I remained alert, still expecting Modocs to appear. But in the surrounding gallyways soldiers' voices were raised in awe as they realized, after six long months of perdition, the Stronghold was now theirs.

I came to a small area encircled by piled rocks. In the center, were the ashes of a fire. This place must have been where the scalps of Canby and Thomas had been flaunted as Indians shuffled round in a victory dance. Then, as they celebrated their victories, the air had throbbed with drumbeats and chanting — now, there was only eerie silence.

Presently I heard the shouted commands of noncoms as they restored discipline, ordering their men to fortify their positions in case the Modocs returned.

Army cooks arrived from Hospital Rock and set up their Dutch-ovens. At this time Gillem came in from the main camp to take command, and presently an orderly found me and requested my presence at Jack's cave. 'They got a prisoner,' the orderly told me.

When I stepped down into the cave, I found a group of officers standing round an old Modoc woman. I didn't know her. She was trembling with fear.

Gillem turned to me and said, 'The Warm Spring Indians have admitted they heard voices last night coming from the south east of the Stronghold. For some foolish reason they didn't report it to their officers. See what this woman says. Ask her how the Modocs escaped from this place.'

As I translated Gillem's questions, the mystery began to unfold.

The woman revealed that the Modocs had suffered only two casualties during the entire five months they had been under siege. Two boys had gone to investigate a cannon ball that had failed to explode on landing. As they poked it, it went off, blowing them to bits.

'Last night Jack decide to quit

Stronghold,' she explained. 'The spirits speak to him, say now is good time to go.'

She related how a few sharpshooters lingered to keep the army occupied, while the remaining Modocs — warriors, women and children — escaped down a lava gully on the eastern side of the Stronghold, walking as quietly as possible.

Gillem's face flushed with anger. 'Eastern side of the Stronghold! They must've passed between Green's and Mason's men — a gap of no more than five hundred yards. If the Warm Springs heard sounds, why the hell didn't they report it?'

'If the Modocs had been caught right then,' somebody said, 'the Warm Springs would've been out of a paid job!'

The old woman was talking again. 'Hours after Jack escaped, the rear-guard also pulled out, this time in broad daylight. They followed along the same trail as the main group.'

The escape of the Indians was a disgrace, and Gillem knew it. He was silent for a moment, no doubt wondering how he was going to explain matters to his superiors. The other officers stood around, waiting for him to speak. At last he said, 'Gentlemen, we will not let the Indians' escape overshadow the fact that we have achieved a great victory. We have dislodged the Modocs from their Stronghold. Our losses have been small.'

'The only trouble,' Major Green remarked, 'is that we don't know where our defeated enemy has gone. They'll be even more dangerous to the local population now they're roaming across the land.'

Gillem glared at Green, then turned to Captain Perry. 'David, take a mounted patrol of fifty men and make a circuit of the Lava Beds. Try to establish if the Modocs are still around.'

As Perry hurried away, the colonel swung round to face Major Green. 'Until we know the position of the

Indians, I want this camp in the Stronghold maintained, as well as our camps at Hospital Rock, Scorpion Point and at main-base. The Warm Springs Indians are to camp at Ticknor Point. These camps must guard the lake shore and stop the Modocs getting water.'

Green nodded and the gathering broke up.

An hour later the snap of a pistol shot echoed along the Stronghold trenches. I joined the general rush towards the spot where the sound had come from, and there we found Major Green crouching on the ground, holding his head as blood streamed through his fingers. Close by, was a sheepish looking captain with a revolver in his hand. 'Damned gun,' he said. 'Discharged by mistake!'

Green scowled at the young officer, his voice full of scorn. 'A few months ago, the Modocs blazed away at me and missed. Now, one of my own officers has done a better job!'

The bullet had grazed his temple, leaving a bloody groove. A fraction closer and it would have blown out his brains.

The captain was stammering his apologies as Green was helped away to get medical attention.

Next day Ed Muybridge set up his tripods and photographed smiling officers, soldiers and Warm Springs Indians strolling along the lava trenches, posing on the stone shelters they'd erected.

Newspapermen flocked into the Stronghold. The soldiers obliged them to the hilt, exaggerating their stories beyond plausibility.

That afternoon, we heard shots coming from the direction of main-camp. From the ramparts, we gazed over the lava rock to see a scurry of movement and the white puff of gun smoke between us and Gillem's Bluff. The air was strangely still, and we heard Modoc voices directing profanity towards the men in the base-camp.

I raised some field glasses bringing

the distant figures into focus. I recognized the red bandanna of Scarfaced Charley. He was leading an attack. On his command, the Indians were discharging their guns into the air so that the bullets went skyward before falling onto the army tents in the base-camp at Gillem's Bluff.

'It's Charley's idea of a joke,' I said to the head-bandaged Major Green who'd come up alongside me. 'They're mimicking army mortars. Trouble is they might just kill somebody.'

The soldiers at Gillem's Camp did not retaliate. The Modoc bombardment went on for an hour and then, as darkness seeped in, the firing ceased and the Indians faded away, vanishing into the vastness of the land. I hoped that Toby had not been harmed.

The attack, albeit by a small party, showed that although the Modocs had quit the Stronghold, they had no intention of giving up the fight. Still worried about Toby, I set out on foot, next morning, for Gillem's Camp. I traveled with F Troop that was returning to get supplies. We marched by a roundabout route and on the way we discovered the body of a young civilian packer who'd been delivering cartridges to the military. The Indians had slashed his belly, letting his bowels out. They'd also flattened his head between two rocks. I sensed this was the work of Hooker Jim. It somehow bore his grisly trademark.

When we reached Gillem's Camp, we found the guards alert in case the Modocs reappeared.

As I rushed through the tents, I met a corporal who was walking towards the camp's cemetery. He was carrying a small coffin.

'You got a baby in there?' I enquired.

He shook his head. 'It's Sergeant Gode's leg. Doc cut it off yesterday. The sergeant 'specially asked that it was buried alongside his pals.'

I nodded and didn't delay him, but hastened to the hospital tent. Here, I found Toby, weary but unharmed. The heavily bandaged Meacham was sitting up on his cot smoking his pipe, looking surprisingly cheerful.

'I figure,' he said, 'the Lord put my hair in the right places — all bushy whiskers with nothing on top of my head. If it'd been the other way round, Boston Charley would have yanked off my scalp.' He grimaced as a spasm of pain shot through him. 'I'm a Christian,' he said, 'and I can forgive most of the Modocs for what they did . . . but I can never forgive Jack. He could have stopped all this.'

He lay back, regathering his strength and thoughts, then said, 'Fifty desperate Indians are striking terror through the entire population. It's impossible for the army to guard every homestead.'

Toby rested her hand on my shoulder. 'Frank, Meacham's going to his home tomorrow. D'you mind if I go with him. Him mighty sick. He needs me to nurse him.'

I felt a twinge of jealousy. Damn it, she was my wife! But then I cursed myself for being selfish. I guess she'd more than earned herself a respite from this war. I gave her a reluctant nod.

Next day, I stood on the jetty as Meacham and Toby prepared to embark. There was a storm blowing up and the lake was pretty rough, but the skipper of the boat reckoned they would make it.

Toby came and put her arms around me. 'We catch stage from Lost River,' she said, 'then we go to Meacham's house in Salem.'

I kissed her farewell and soon the boat was being rowed out onto the lake.

After they'd gone, the storm turned real bad and I was worried sick, but in the morning the boat returned. The outgoing journey had been completed safely, though everybody had been 'mightily seasick'.

I stayed at Gillem's Camp.

Captain Perry's company returned from its patrol of the Lava Beds and within an hour Gillem had called a conference of officers. 'Gentlemen,' he said, his old swagger restored, 'Captain Perry has engaged no Modocs but he reckons they're camped somewhere in Schonchin Flow, about four miles to the south.' He used a stick to point at the large map he had displayed.

'I believe that we must shell the enemy into submission, rather than chase him all over the country. We'll send out another reconnaissance patrol, just to make sure.' He turned to me. 'I want you to go as scout. Nobody else knows the area better than you, Mister Riddle.'

Had I guessed the forthcoming nightmare, I would have refused the duty, but foolishly I nodded my acceptance.

13

Captain Evan Thomas gleefully rubbed his hands together as his patrol formed up. He was a tall man with bushy sideburns and thick wavy hair. He reminded me of a horse champing at the bit.

'Well, Mister Riddle,' he said, 'I've missed all the action so far, but now at least I've got a patrol to lead out, though unfortunately we're not to attack the Modocs.'

I finished chewing my breakfast of greasy salt pork and wiped my hands on my britches. My sentiments were different from the captain's. I hoped I'd never hear another shot fired in anger.

It was 7 o'clock and in the clear morning light we could see our objective some six miles to the south — the large, treeless Sand Butte. It was here that Gillem wished to place his artillery.

I walked down the column to where the burly packer Louis Webber was strapping supplies onto his five mules. These were the only animals we were taking. Horses were useless over the rough terrain.

'I hear we're gonna link up with McKay and his scouts,' Webber commented.

'They're coming from Ticknor Point,' I said. 'They plan to meet us at Sand Butte round about noon.'

Webber glanced to where the officers were standing. 'All them officers are new out here,' he commented. 'You'd have thought Gillem would've assigned at least one experienced Indian fighter.'

I shared his uneasiness. I knew Gillem viewed this as a routine reconnaissance.

'Gillem wants Thomas to check out possible gun positions,' I said, 'then come back. He figures the Modocs are in that lava flow to the east.'

Thomas ordered us forward. We had some sixty men. Two officers, Thomas and the white-haired Lieutenant Wright followed close behind the center of the skirmish line, and as we progressed, I joined them. Wright looked quite old for his junior rank. I wondered why he hadn't been given a desk job. Behind us came the artillery batteries in column of twos, led by Lieutenants Harris and Howe. At the rear of the column were Webber's laden mules and a rearguard of four men under Lieutenant Cranston. Doctor Bernard Semig plodded alongside them.

Thomas was irritated by the slow progress. During the first hour we scarcely covered a mile. He ordered the pace quickened, but the men made no effort to speed up and as we marched, the sun rose before us, causing men to shield their eyes.

Lieutenant Wright was breathing heavily and sometimes stopped to mop his brow. 'Bloody hot for this time of year,' he complained.

'That's the trouble,' Thomas responded. 'This country can be tropical one moment, and freezing the next.'

No flankers had been deployed to watch for Indians. I felt unhappy about this and told Captain Thomas so.

'Indians must be at least eighteen miles away,' he scoffed.

'You can't rely on that,' I insisted. 'Look at the way Scarfaced Charley came back. He caused plenty of trouble.'

'All right, Mister Riddle,' Thomas sighed and he ordered men out, but the ground on each side of the lava flow, along which we walked, was cross-ridged, so that men were obliged to constantly climb and descend. This was so tiring that they converged back towards the main column. Lieutenant Cranston shouted at them to move out but they ignored him. The unfledged officers seemed not to realize how vulnerable we were to ambush. The situation depressed me.

We kept looking to the north for sight

of McKay and his Indian scouts. When we stopped to rest, we spotted them — small dots in the far distance, but their pace was even slower than ours.

As we continued, we passed between two high shoulders of lava flow. Around us, the ground was broken by knobs of lava that jutted up every few yards. Thick bunch grass grew knee-high, concealing small, razor-edged stones.

About 11 o'clock we passed beyond a high ridge and could no longer see Gillem's Bluff.

'They won't be able to keep track of us from Signal Rock now,' Sergeant Romer commented.

I nodded. 'In about an hour we'll be on higher ground. We'll be able to make contact again.'

The sun was almost directly overhead and our shirts were dark with sweat. Noon saw us on the west side of Sand Butte, which was about two hundred feet high. I remembered it had a great hollow on its crest that could easily conceal Indians.

The ground rose and fell, sometimes plunging us so low that we couldn't see our surroundings. But later when we crested the more elevated points, we could see Gillem's Bluff again — and hopefully the signalers could see us.

To the east, the sullen rocks of Schonchin Flow loomed some twenty feet high — and in the south, the ground was bordered by a series of low, jagged bluffs. We were about a half-mile from Sand Butte. We reached a point where desert-mahogany shrubs provided tempting shade and Captain Thomas ordered a halt.

'We'll wait till McKay turns up,' he said.

'We're too overlooked here,' I warned him. 'This place is a perfect trap.'

Arrogance flared in his eyes. He didn't answer.

There may have been some sentries out. I can't recall. Men stacked their guns and slumped down, unloading their packs and rations, reaching for their canteens. Some removed their boots and rubbed their weary, blistered feet.

Meanwhile, Thomas motioned Lieutenant Harris and me to join him. 'Let's climb up there,' he said, pointing to the bluff on the southern side. 'We'll signal Gillem's Camp, let 'em know there are no Modocs around.'

'We may not see them,' I said. 'That doesn't mean they're not around.'

'No Indians are going to attack sixty well-armed men.'

'Canby had that same confidence!' I snapped back at him.

He gave me a dismissive wave, then ordered a signal-corporal with his flags to accompany us. He led the way towards the bluff. Everywhere was quiet, apart from the voices of the reclining soldiers. Lieutenant Cranston and a few men were clambering up the bluff on the opposite side to us. We started to climb.

We'd gone about thirty paces when gunfire shattered the hush.

In alarm, we gazed across to the

opposite bluff, saw the orange flash of more shots coming from its crest. Cranston and three of his men had fallen.

Thomas turned to his signaler and shouted, 'Send a message back to camp. Tell them we've located the Indians!'

Unfurling his flags, the signaler climbed higher and conveyed his message, relying on field glasses at Gillem's Bluff to pick him up. Meanwhile, down below, soldiers were scrambling to reach their stacked guns. Suddenly a second blast of heavier fire cut through them, and officers were shouting at them to make a stand. Webber's mules had broken free, braying loudly, stampeding.

Captain Wright and a few of his men advanced up the far slope into the face of bullets, returning fire as they went. But suddenly, Wright went down and his men turned and ran. There was a general panic. Rations, even weapons, were dropped as men fled over the rough lava.

I had a brief glimpse of Modocs firing from the far skyline. Some soldiers were shot down.

I looked northward, praying for sight of McKay and his scouts. Instead, I saw more Modocs surging over the crest of Sand Butte.

To the east was a hollow filled with sage brush and rocks. Doctor Semig and some enlisted men had taken cover there and were directing fire at the Indians.

Thomas shouted. 'Let's get down there!' and we made a dash, kicking our way through the cinders. Bullets whined and chipped the rocks near us.

As we ran, the signal-corporal cried out, 'Oh my God!'

I turned and saw him go down, dropping his flags with a clatter. I stumbled across and stood over him. He'd been shot through the chest. He looked up at me, tried to speak, but instead of words, blood seeped from his mouth, and in that moment his eyes glazed over and I knew he was beyond help. I left him.

As we reached the hollow, Thomas himself was shot. He fell, but pulled himself into a sitting position, blood soaking his shirt. He attempted to knock a percussion cap from the cylinder of his revolver, but the gun exploded, leaving his hand looking like fire-blackened meat. I tried to drag him behind cover, but he pushed me off, seemingly oblivious to pain. 'I'll not retreat,' he cried out. 'This is as good a place as any to die!' And then he turned to what was left of his command and shouted, 'Men, we're surrounded. We must fight and die like soldiers.' Then another bullet struck him.

I fired off several shots to shield him, anger surging through me, but when I looked at him again he was dead. Maybe he'd been crazy to get us ambushed — but he'd surely died a hero.

A bullet burned the air close to my cheek. I ducked behind the boulders.

For a moment there was a lull in

firing. I became aware of a man's groans and, turning, I saw Doctor Bernard Semig. He'd been shot in the foot. He was doubled up with pain.

'There's no hope for me,' he groaned. 'If I don't bleed to death, I'll die of gangrene.'

'You're not dead yet,' I said.

Semig cursed, his face deathly white. 'Riddle, do you think I'm a complete fool? I'm a doctor!'

'Where's McKay?' a Sergeant Oliver murmured. 'He's the only one who can save us.'

I shook my head.

I tried to take stock of our surroundings. There were probably about twenty of us in these boulders but many were wounded and the shelter was so scant that once the Modocs renewed their attack, we would stand little chance.

Across the basin, I could see Indians crouched over bodies, stripping off clothes, finding ammunition and guns.

I recognized the muscular figure of Hooker Jim. He was working with a slab of rock, pounding at a man's head, fiendishly flattening it in the same way he had young Hovey's. Hooker Jim had set this country aflame by killing the settlers. He had forced Jack's hand by seeking protection from him, and he had butchered men as if they were hogs

I raised my rifle, drawing a bead on him — but I didn't pull the trigger. Sergeant Oliver gasped, 'Why don't you shoot?'

I lowered my weapon. 'It'd bring them down on our heads like a pack of wolves.'

I cursed McKay. He'd disappeared somewhere. It was unlikely that he'd help us now. Furthermore, it would be hours before the dithering Gillem would have a relief force here. I wondered how many of our men had run off. It was six miles to the camp across lava — and with Modocs in pursuit, their prospects wouldn't be good.

Suddenly, the Indians who'd crossed the crest of Sand Butte opened fire.

Lead whined spitefully through our inadequate cover, bringing cries of pain and fear from our huddled men. Yet even so they managed to fire back, and I heard an officer bravely encouraging his men to aim carefully.

But the only outcome was that our enemies took cover behind rocks and subjected us to even greater bombardment. Several times I heard the sickly thud of lead hitting flesh, and the shocked, sudden intake of a man's breath.

The Indian fire rose deafeningly and then tapered off. They seemed to be all around us. If they rushed us now, we would be finished. But they replaced bullets with shouted taunts. They called us every obscenity imaginable. Above us the sky had darkened, the temperature dropped and rain started to fall. A corporal was sprawled close to me, the side of his head bleeding. Behind me in the boulders, I didn't know how many men were in any condition to defend themselves. Semig had lost consciousness.

I noticed that the Indians had ceased their taunting. There was a strange hush, broken only by the groaning of wounded men.

Suddenly a soldier called that there were Modocs creeping across the rocks on the north. I couldn't see from my position, but some of our men opened fire and apparently drove them back.

'They're just bidin' their time,' somebody groaned. 'They'll wait till it's dark, then they'll get us.'

I peered through the squally rain, not seeing any movement out there — and then we heard a bugle-call and our spirits rose. But there was something strange about those notes. They lacked the normal smoothness; they were hesitant, uneven.

Sergeant Oliver cursed. 'It's an Injun blowing that,' he groaned.

Shots blasted out from our men on the northern side of the boulders. They had again spotted Indians sneaking up on us, and for a moment we all prepared ourselves for the final onslaught. I heard a man praying aloud . . . but then the shots trailed off. 'Driven 'em away, thank God!' somebody murmured.

Gloomy darkness began to take hold.

Those next hours were dismal. Men lay bleeding as icy rain washed over them, dead bodies beside them.

Semig had regained consciousness but he was delirious. I eased his boot off. I found his bag of field-dressings and extracted some bandage and bound up his bloody foot as best I could. Then I crawled through the boulders, doing what I could for the other wounded — but in the darkness my hands were slippery with either blood or water, I couldn't be sure which. I counted seven men still alive, all wounded except three.

As I returned to my original position, I heard a sound coming from the bluff on the south side — the clink of rocks being piled one upon the other. 'Sounds as if the Modocs are building some sort of shelter,' Sergeant Oliver whispered. 'God knows why!'

For a long time we lay, numbed with cold, listening to the sound. It carried on the wind, strangely eerie. Then, faintly, I caught the brief murmur of voices.

I made up my mind. There seemed little point in waiting till the morning. I put my mouth close to Sergeant Oliver's ear. 'Maybe it's our people out there. I'm going to see.'

'You're crazy,' he gasped, but he was too exhausted to comment further.

Stiffly, I rose to my feet. *Please God*, I murmured beneath my breath. '*Please God . . .* ' but then I thought of the Reverend Thomas. All the praying he'd done hadn't kept him alive. The wind and rain were buffeting my face. I turned my head to the side, took a deep breath, then stepped out from the boulders into the darkness.

14

I figured my gamble presented our only chance of survival. But, in honesty, with Indians roaming over the area, I was most likely to end up being butchered — or alternatively, if soldiers were camped somewhere up there in the rocks, I would prove the ideal target for a panicky trooper.

For what seemed hours, I crawled over the sharp lava, the wind and freezing rain punishing me. My hands and knees were cut and scraped raw. There was no moon and the blackness was thick. At last I reached a gradient. This had to be the beginning of the south bluff.

Soon, my fingers clawed into something soft. It was a naked, lifeless body. In the darkness, I had no means of identifying it, nor had I the stomach to try. But I knew that here must be one of the men who, only a few hours earlier, had marched alongside me from Gillem's Camp. As I crouched over him, I took strange solace in his company. I was, for a brief moment, no longer completely alone.

Then the noise came again, snatched to me on the wind's bluster, the thud of rock against rock, and with it, the muted, anxious sound of a voice issuing orders. I slumped down, my heart hammering with relief.

At last, I scrambled up and with the most resolution I could muster, I hurled my voice into the wind: 'I am Frank Riddle, a survivor from Captain Thomas's command! Don't shoot!'

I strained my ears, cursing the muffling effect of the wind. Maybe my senses had tricked me.

Again, I yelled out: 'Don't shoot. I'm Frank Riddle!'

This time a Kentucky voice responded: 'Come on up, mister. Any tricks an' you're dead!'

No invitation ever sounded sweeter.

Ten minutes later, I'd been led through the line of rock shelters the men had built, and I was hearing the familiar cursing of Major Johnny Green. With him, hunkered down in the darkness, was Lieutenant Boutelle.

Breathlessly, I related the tragic events. 'Thomas, Wright and most of the command . . . ambushed and killed. A few survivors, wounded men . . . down there in the basin. My God, they're desperate for medical help.'

Green kept clicking his tongue in dismay. At last he said. 'We had no idea how serious the situation was. Gillem was sure the patrol was strong enough to look after itself.'

'When some survivors got back to camp,' Boutelle cut in, 'we started out, but the weather had turned bad and it was getting dark.'

'We didn't have a competent guide,' Green explained as he chewed on some hard tack. 'We got lost, had no idea where we were. It was pointless going further, so we camped here.'

'You stopped just a few yards from where your help was needed,' I gasped. I felt angry. 'Those wounded men down there. They need a doctor now!'

Green hesitated, then said, 'We'll wait till daylight. With Modocs still around, it would be crazy to leave our positions here.'

'But Semig and the rest of them are dying,' I argued. 'They need a doctor before it's too late.'

'We don't have a doctor,' Green admitted. 'We knew you had Semig with you and . . . '

I swore with exasperation.

'Come daylight,' Green said, 'we'll signal for medical aid. Try and get some rest now. Tomorrow will be a harrowing day.'

For what was left of that stormy, black night, I sheltered behind a rock wall. Each time I closed my eyes, images flooded before me, images of men being shot down, their faces contorted in agony.

Dawn eventually came, gray, bleak

and bitterly cold, so different from the clear day of yesterday!

I stood up and gazed beyond the rocky breastworks. In the gloom, the basin looked forlorn. Nothing moved. If Modocs were around, they were hiding. I wondered if Semig, Lieutenant Harris, Sergeant Oliver and the others still survived. I tried to spot the hollow where I had left them. I couldn't. It would have to be found on foot.

Lieutenant Boutelle appeared and said, 'Mister Riddle, I'm taking a detail out to search for survivors. I'd appreciate your assistance.'

I nodded.

Ten minutes later, we left the breastworks with a detail of a dozen men and advanced down the bluff. The first body we encountered was that of a young private. This must have been the body I'd encountered during the darkness. The sight of him, stripped, mutilated, had some of the men turning their backs, sickened — but more hideous sights awaited us.

Boutelle remained his efficient self, warning his men to keep a watch for Indians. We combed through the rocks and more bodies were located in the crevices. Suddenly we heard weak cries for help, and I realized we were approaching the hollow. We discovered the bodies of Captain Thomas and Lieutenant Howe. Then we moved down into the depression and found Doctor Semig, Lieutenant Harris, Sergeant Oliver and four enlisted men. All were still breathing, but suffering terrible wounds. Boutelle immediately sent a runner back to Green, requesting stretchers and water.

The wounded Sergeant Oliver and two other men were able to walk from the hollow unaided — but Lieutenant Harris, who'd been shot in the back, had to be lifted onto a stretcher, as did several others. These men had been through hell. If they retained their sanity it would be a miracle.

We searched the basin for the living,

but we found only dismembered corpses.

The dreary morning slipped by. I stood guard as men worked with their spades and lowered the bodies of their former comrades into shallow graves. The remains of the officers were carried back to the bluff, there to await conveyance to home-town cemeteries, so that they could be buried with the dignity befitting their social status.

Suddenly, on the crest of Sand Butte, Indians appeared, gazing at us and waving their guns. They were out of rifle range, but it wouldn't take them long to get closer. Our men paused in their tasks.

Boutelle approached me, his revolver in his hand. 'D'you think they'll attack us?' he asked.

I nodded. 'We should fall back to the bluff. I don't think we'll find anybody else left alive.'

Boutelle agreed. His men needed no second bidding to withdraw.

But as we returned across the basin,

a shout went up and gazing to the north we saw Donald McKay and his Warm Spring Indians threading their way through the lava towards us. As the rest of our detail climbed towards the shelter of the rock forts, I waited for the slow-moving scouts. McKay reached me, giving a weary wave of his hand.

'Where the hell have you been?' I asked.

He took off his hat, ran a hand through his hair. 'We tried to help,' he explained, 'but every time we got near, those sojers opened fire on us. My boys waved their hats in the air to show we was friendly. We even blew a bugle to prove we weren't Modocs. But all we got was damned bullets!'

I'd never imagined war could be so crazy.

We climbed the bluff and went through the line of rock forts.

Green came up to me. 'We'll wait till it's dark before we move out. At least we've got you to guide us this time, Mister Riddle.'

It was three o'clock before Doctor McElderry and his two orderlies arrived, having been summoned by Major Green's signaler. They were carrying weighty packs of medical supplies on their shoulders. 'Damn well got lost,' the doctor explained, dumping his load thankfully down. 'Those lava flows are a complete maze. Our mules wouldn't cross the ridges, so we abandoned them and carried the packs ourselves.'

'Well, thank God you're here,' Green said. 'There's plenty of work for you.'

Soon McElderry was administering to the wounded, but the lack of water made things desperate.

I couldn't stave off my own weariness any longer. Green had allowed his men to light fires, and finding a warm spot I eased my boots off and rested down.

At last the day's light faded, and Green gave the order to move out. One of the wounded ceased his agonized cries and there was a delay while McElderry checked his pulse and directed that the body should be left beneath piled rocks. That left nine stretchers to be carried.

We progressed across rocks and gulches, men glancing over their shoulders, fearing attack. Green was relying on me not to lose the way, but in the dusk this became more difficult. The twelve Warm Spring Indians kept at the head of the column, though they were unfamiliar with the country and gave me no assistance. Behind us, the command formed an extended line, disappearing into the gloom. Mules were carrying the bodies of the dead officers. As we advanced, we often had to roll boulders aside to clear the trail.

Suddenly gunfire crackled from behind us. Down the line, everybody dropped to the ground, seeking cover behind rocks as weapons were made ready.

The gunfire ceased. For a moment the only sound was the braying of mules.

'Modocs are trailing us,' Boutelle

said, as he crouched near me, revolver drawn, 'but they're some way back, I guess.'

I nodded. We didn't wait long before Green ordered us forward again.

Now, driving sleet added to our misery, driving into us in gusts of freezing torture. I felt numbed to the bone, having worn only light clothes when we'd set out in the sunshine of yesterday. Noncoms pleaded and cajoled to keep their men moving.

I was guiding the column by blind instinct, my eyes watering tears that stiffened my cheeks with ice. We angled towards the southwest. Green walked beside me, moving back occasionally to check the column. It must have been an hour later that we again saw the glimmer of distant fires. Green called a halt as we conferred.

'Could be Indians again,' he said.

I tried to take stock of our position. 'More likely beacons burning on top of Gillem's Bluff,' I said.

'Then we're getting close to camp,'

Green murmured.

'We better not make direct for those beacons,' I said. 'We'd blunder into deep craters. We'll never get across there in the dark. We've got to keep going north for another mile or so.'

'Very well, Mister Riddle,' Green sighed. 'We're in your hands.'

As we moved on, Boutelle, who seemed to be everywhere, reported that several men had deserted, preferring to blunder their way back alone.

We reached Gillem's Camp at six-thirty, just as dawn's icy fingers were probing the eastern sky. The journey had taken an awful toll. We were all frozen, coated with ice. For my own part, I couldn't stop shaking.

The tortured, pallid faces of the wounded were terrible. They were resigned to death. Most of them had ceased their groans and some were unconscious. I saw Semig's eyes moving. Lieutenant Harris looked dead. Doctor McElderry pulled back his blanket listened for a heart beat. 'He's still in this world,' he gasped, 'but that's a miracle.'

I nodded and then I looked ahead and saw men rushing from their tents to meet us and support us over the last few yards to safety. The wounded were taken from their exhausted bearers, and men spoke in shocked, respectful whispers as news of the tragedy was passed by word of mouth.

I could do little more than find my tent, wrap myself in a blanket and collapse. How I wished dear Toby was here! During the next hours, my shaking grew worse. All the fear, all the closeness to death, was taking hold of me, like rats gnawing at my soul.

I recall forcing myself up to vomit, and of bending over with griping pains in my guts . . . and later being only half conscious as I was carried into the post hospital and dosed with laudanum.

15

Rest gradually restored my strength, melted the iciness from my bones. On the fourth evening of my stay in the post hospital, we were given canned apricots for supper. 'With the compliments of the ladies of Yreka,' an orderly announced. 'The new commander, Colonel Davis, brought a supply with him when he arrived.'

Next day the colonel himself visited the hospital tent on a tour of inspection. Colonel Gillem was with him.

Davis was a hard man, you could see that from the start. His eyes had the paleness of ice. He was not impressed by our jittery command. Looking at me, he said, 'Mister Riddle, I trust you will soon be fit. I believe you are very much needed.'

On the afternoon of the following

day, the rancher John Fairchild paid a visit. He brought me a box of cheroots. As we lit up, he said, 'Davis is confident Indians won't return to the Stronghold, so he's abandoned the camp there.'

Fairchild had had a long talk with Davis. He had learned that Davis also intended to give up Gillem's Camp and move his headquarters to the Fairchild ranch.

If I needed something to speed my recovery, I got it next day. Toby returned with news that Meacham was on the mend. Now she fussed me and just having her near lifted my spirits no end. She was everything a man could wish in his woman.

And so it was. Within a week, I was back on my feet and watching the army set up its tents and equipment in the meadows surrounding Fairchild's ranch house. Meanwhile, more patrols were going out, probing into the Lava Beds. Plenty of food, medical supplies and water were always taken, the hard lessons of the past having been learned.

One afternoon, Major Mason came back with news that he'd found evidence of the Modocs recently sheltering in some ice caves. They'd chipped away at the ice to obtain water.

'Davis isn't engaging the Modocs,' Fairchild commented one evening over supper, 'but he's sure hounding them. They keep on the run, just ahead of the soldiers all the time. But lack of rest will eventually wear them down, particularly the women and kids. Then maybe Jack will give up.'

Next day, a patrol returned to Fairchild's with two Modoc women as prisoners.

I helped Colonel Davis as he questioned one of the captives — One Eyed Dixie. In Davis's big bell tent, she talked quite willingly, clearly thankful she didn't have to run from the soldiers any longer.

She told us that there'd been a squabble amongst the Modocs. 'Hooker Jim blame Jack for quitting the Stronghold. There was big row. Many

Modocs tired of fighting, want to give up. Too much moving and no water get everybody down. So Hooker Jim, thirteen men and their families split from Jack's band and ride west to head of Butte Valley.

'And where's Jack and what's left of his band gone?'

She hesitated, then said, 'Camped some place at edge of lava flows.'

Davis was pleased with this information. He sat pondering for a while. Eventually he turned to me. 'I want her to find the Modocs and tell them to surrender. If they surrender we will treat them as prisoners-of-war. If they don't surrender, we'll shoot them all!'

I translated his words and One Eyed Dixie nodded.

She was gone for five days. I'd wondered if we had seen the last of her, but my fears were ungrounded. When One Eyed Dixie rode into camp, she came straight to me. 'Hooker Jim say they give up if Fairchild goes by himself to meet them. They trust Fairchild, nobody else.' I nodded and immediately reported the news to Fairchild.

'Nobody's said whether Hooker Jim will stand trial for murdering the settlers,' Fairchild observed. 'I bet Davis won't let him get away with it.'

'Will you go to meet Hooker Jim's band?' I asked.

'I'll do anything to help bring peace to this country,' Fairchild said.

He knew full well that he might be walking into a death trap, but he was determined to go. He left early next morning, riding out alone.

In the evening of that day, a Warm Spring scout reported that Fairchild was leading a band of Modocs in. Maybe a hundred troops, together with the usual hangers on, gathered to watch the surrender, but they were disappointed. Fairchild arrived with only a few warriors and their families. They looked sullen as they rode between lines of soldiers. Their faces were blackened with charcoal. Some of the men were wearing tattered army uniforms, stolen from the bodies of killed soldiers. The women were wearing dresses no doubt plundered from the cabins of murdered settlers. The privation suffered by the tribe was reflected in the sorry state of their horses. They were walking rib cages, hobbling along on split hooves and sagging beneath the weight of their burdens.

Colonel Davis awaited the Indians, his face showing no emotion. Fairchild led the column right up to him and called a halt. Striving to retain their dignity, the warriors dismounted and laid their rifles at the colonel's feet. It was an uncanny sight. Bogus led the way, the usual grin absent from his lips; the tall Steamboat Frank and Shack-nasty Jim followed him. Then came the shaman Curly Headed Doctor, his magic power broken.

'Where's Hooker Jim?' Davis demanded.

'Hooker Jim dead,' Bogus replied. 'So too Boston Charley.'

Davis nodded, then invited the four

leaders into his tent. I followed to interpret. Backed by armed guards, Davis sat behind his field desk. He pushed his hat back with his index finger, then asked the Indians about the whereabouts of Jack and the others.

All at once there was an alarmed shouting from outside. Most of us turned as the tent flap was ripped open. A panting Indian burst in and threw himself face-down on the ground in front of the colonel's desk. Guards rushed in, would have grabbed the Indian, but Davis waved them aside. He stood up, paced around the desk and towered over the groveling Modoc. The latter lifted his head, met the colonel's eye — and I saw his face.

'That's Hooker Jim,' I told Davis.

'Ask him why he didn't come in with the others,' Davis requested, and I translated.

He replied meekly. 'I stay outside of camp to see if other Modocs were shot by soldiers. When I see they were not shot, I come.'

'He ran through all the sentries to reach my tent,' Davis commented angrily. 'He could've killed me before anybody batted an eyelid.'

But Hooker Jim had craftier plans. 'I know where Captain Jack hides,' he said. 'If soldier-chief promise I will not be punished for killing settlers, I will show soldiers where Jack is camped.'

As I translated, Davis hesitated. The only sound was the panting breath of Hooker Jim.

Suddenly the decision was made and Davis nodded. 'Find me Jack, convince him to give up, and we'll treat you as a prisoner-of-war.'

'Colonel!' I gasped. 'Hooker Jim is a murderer many times over. He took part in the murder of General Canby and Reverend Thomas. He killed those settlers last November, then turned to Jack for protection. Now he's ready to betray him. He deserves a noose more than anybody else in this war!'

'Hooker Jim is a reformed Indian, Mr Riddle,' Davis responded.

I held my tongue, too disgusted to say more.

Only then did Hooker Jim come to his feet, a satisfied smirk on his savage face.

The Modoc War had taken yet another crazy turn.

16

In readiness for prisoners, Davis had ordered tents erected close to the creek. Each tent contained an ample supply of blankets. Beef and coffee were provided — the first decent meal the Indians had had in days.

Toby wandered among her people, talking to her relatives over their campfires.

Later, as we ate our own supper, she told me what she'd learned. 'Jack did not want to kill Canby or any of the peace commissioners, but he was forced into it by Hooker Jim and others. At a council in the Stronghold, they call Jack a woman, not worthy to be chief. They throw a shawl over his head, trip him up as he stumbled around. This make Jack very angry. He hurl shawl away. He say he not coward. He say if they want him to kill Canby, then he will do it!

'Later,' Toby went on, 'Jack sorry he make promise. No good come if he kill Canby. But Hooker Jim say Jack must keep promise.'

'I always knew Hooker Jim was the worst of them all.'

'Afterwards,' Toby said, 'Jack plead with rest of tribe. He say all those who want him to kill Canby must stand up. All against it stay sitting. Everybody except Scarfaced Charley and a few others got to their feet. Most of the people believe killing Canby make good revenge for what Ben Wright did to the Modocs.'

'So the deed was done,' I sighed, 'and Jack has been dubbed a bloodthirsty murderer by the entire nation. And Hooker Jim is avoiding justice like a slippery snake.'

       ★ ★ ★

A week later I was summoned to the colonel's headquarters-tent. 'Mister Riddle,' Davis said, waving me to a chair, 'I'm going to move camp to Peninsula Rock. That'll put us closer to the country where Jack is hidden up. And I'm going to transfer the Modoc prisoners there. Major Mason has set up a decent prison camp and we can mount a proper guard.'

'Good,' I said. 'That'll keep the Modocs in, and any troublemakers out.'

He nodded. 'You've got the reputation of being the best interpreter in the territory. I want to end this war, to do that I've got to track Jack down. There may be some delicate negotiations to undertake. I need you.'

'Yes,' I murmured bitterly, 'you need me to help hound him to the gallows.'

Right then I sensed I was trapped, just like Jack was. We all had to follow what destiny held for us. We had no real choice.

'We haven't found the exact location of Jack's camp yet,' Davis continued, 'but I'm making Hooker Jim and his friends earn their pay, guiding patrols, checking out all the camp-sites they know.'

The new Peninsula Camp was shadowed by a rock bluff. It rose from the lake, linked to the mainland by a narrow neck of land. The tented prison camp was at the foot of the bluff, the way to the mainland blocked by the fortified army encampment.

The number of army patrols going out was increased. Gradually the Indian threat was being scaled down. Modocs, mostly women, children and old people were found in separate camps, waiting to give themselves up. They were exhausted. All they wanted was food, water and rest. The army promptly obliged.

I hated Hooker Jim and even standing near him made me feel sick, but I had to interpret his words for Davis. 'Not many left in Jack's band. With him now are his two wives, his young daughter and a few other relatives. Then there'll be John Schonchin, Scarfaced Charley, their families and maybe a half-dozen bucks.'

'That's more than enough to keep the ranchers pissing their pants,' Davis commented. 'We must catch him as soon as possible.'

Twenty-four hours later, Hooker Jim came in from a scout. 'I find tracks left by Jack's people.' he grinned. 'He has hideout at Willow Creek in the canyon east of Clear Lake.'

Colonel Davis glanced at me, obviously delighted. Now, he moved quickly. Early on the following day, some six weeks after the Modocs had walked out from the Stronghold, two squadrons of mounted troops took to the field and I went with them. In overall command of the two squadrons was Major Jackson, the officer who'd led the bungled attack on the Lost River camp last November. Now, his orders were quite clear. Jack was to be taken, dead or alive. Hooker Jim, Bogus Charley, Steamboat Frank and Shacknasty Jim joined the column as scouts, gloating over their new status.

It was as if we were wolves, going after a wounded buffalo bull. Jack might not have been physically wounded, but his pride, his spirit, had been struck a mortal blow. And one thing was certain. A wounded bull is twice as dangerous as a fit one.

As we progressed, the sun gradually emerged as a searing ball. We skirted the Lava Beds, cursing the dust in the air. We were thankful when we passed into cooler, timbered terrain. We stopped at noon for food and rest. Memories lingered of Thomas's ill-fated expedition, when men had lolled about, but this time things were different. Jackson posted more guards than there were relaxing soldiers.

I glanced across and saw Hooker Jim and the dark skinned Black Jim joking and laughing with some of the younger troopers. These were boys who'd been drafted in since the earlier disasters. They either were unaware of past events or they weren't interested. They figured these Indians were good for a laugh. As always, the passage of time was playing odd tricks!

We reached our destination in the late afternoon.

Willow Creek was a narrow torrent, coming from the hills, flowing into Clear Lake. It rushed through a rocky, fifty-foot-deep gorge. The whole place was a natural hiding place with thick brush.

Our command halted some three miles short of where we figured Jack's camp might be. Hooker Jim and Bogus went forward to scout and presently returned with the news that their surmising was correct.

The command advanced over a rocky, juniper-covered plateau, then Jackson halted and called his officers together. After some discussion he said, 'Gentlemen, we will surround the area where the Modoc camp is and gradually close in.'

Lieutenant Hasbrouck led his men off, intending to carry out these orders, but the rest of us were prevented from putting the plan into immediate effect. As we mounted up, there was a shout and an Indian came walking through the trees with his hands held high, a white cloth fastened to the barrel of his rifle. This was none other than the pint-sized Boston Charley, wearing the suit Reverend Thomas had given him. He now found himself covered by a dozen rifles. He gingerly placed his own weapon on the ground. 'All Modocs are hidden in trees,' he said. 'All want to surrender! Me bring them in if you no shoot.'

We all sensed the end of the war was maybe minutes away. Jackson turned to me. 'Tell him that I promise they will not be harmed if they come forward and lay down their weapons.'

I immediately complied. Boston Charley nodded, turned and walked off into the trees. He was gone maybe fifteen minutes, then he reappeared. 'They come,' he said, gesturing behind him.

Then disaster struck. One of the

Warm Spring scouts, turning his horse in the thick brush, accidentally discharged his rifle. There were alarmed shouts from the approaching Modocs, still concealed in the trees, followed by the sudden, panicking noise of Indians scrambling in retreat.

Jackson was livid, bouncing angrily in his saddle. 'They thought we were shooting at them!' he ranted. 'Now they've scattered like damned quail!'

After he'd simmered down, he told Boston to go and find Jack and convince him all was well. The Indian again disappeared into the trees.

He didn't make it to Jack. We discovered later that he was waylaid by Hasbrouck's men and seized. They didn't know he was on a mission for Jackson, and despite his protestations, he was bound hand and foot.

We waited in vain for his return, and eventually, with the light fast fading we advanced through the trees and in ten minutes came upon what was left of the Modoc encampment — a few wretched blanket-shelters. Waiting there, anxious to surrender, were eight squaws and some children. We also found abandoned equipment and ammunition. But Jack and what was left of his immediate band were gone. The chance to end the war had been bungled.

Jackson ordered the squadrons to make camp for the night.

Next morning, as dawn's deep crimson hung low in the eastern sky, we moved up Willow Creek. Presently the Warm Spring scouts reported that they had located the Modocs' trail heading northward, and we followed this for several miles until it gave out in rocky terrain. For most of the afternoon we scouted for sign, but not until we had crossed a mountain and descended into Langell Valley did the scouts discover tracks again.

In the evening, we spotted three Modoc men ahead of us. The Warm Springs chased them into a sharp canyon near the base of the bluff. One of these men was Scarfaced Charley.

After a moment, as Jackson led the command forward, he walked from his cover with hands held high.

Scarfaced Charley looked downright weary. He said, 'I am tired of fighting. I give up.'

'Where's Jack?' I asked him.

He pointed up the bluff. 'Jack and a few others are on the top. They are worn out. If you want, I will go and talk to Jack and tell him he must give up now.'

As I translated, Jackson nodded.

The Indian plodded up the slope and was soon hidden by the trees.

'Do you think this is a trick, Mister Riddle?' Jackson asked me. 'Maybe they're just playing for time.'

'No,' I said. 'Scarfaced Charley plays things straight, always has done.'

An hour later, Scarfaced Charley reappeared. With him came John Schonchin, and twelve other men, together with their families. They immediately laid down their weapons in front of Major Jackson.

But Jack and several others had not appeared. They'd slipped away over the bluff. 'Jack afraid,' Scarfaced Charley explained, 'but he give up if army promise not to hang him.'

I translated the news to Major Jackson. 'We could give that assurance,' he said, 'but it would not be honest.'

Meanwhile reinforcements had come up, including numerous civilian volunteers, and we made camp for another night. An escort was formed and the prisoners were dispatched to Peninsula Camp.

17

Next day, army columns criss-crossed the country.

I joined Captain Perry, and we scouted the upper Lost River area. We searched the hills for hours without success. Then at last we discovered some tracks, but these scattered in several directions. Perry split his command into detachments, each following separate trails. I went with a Captain Hardeman. We moved along the bluffs on the south side of Willow Creek and eventually reached a point where the canyon swung to the left.

Hardeman and I stood on top of the ravine wall. We studied the terrain through our field glasses. Hardeman spotted a movement on the opposite side of the ravine. We both grunted as we saw a small white dog appear at the head of the ravine. Suddenly an arm reached from the bushes and pulled the dog out of view.

Hardeman gave me a satisfied grin. 'We've found our quarry,' he said, and we set off at a scrambling pace to report to Perry.

Perry immediately concentrated his men along the rims of the ravine. I stayed with Hardeman. We moved over the table-land south of the creek, carefully searching for sign. An hour had gone by since we'd spotted the dog, and we were beginning to think that Jack had once more got away.

But near a bend in the canyon we spotted a small clump of junipers. Some strange instinct warned me that Jack was near.

I advanced with a group of Warm Spring scouts. I felt cold, clammy. We crept through the trees, and presently came upon a dwarf-like Modoc standing with his back to us, gazing at the soldiers on the opposite side of the canyon. We had completely surprised him. The Warm Springs sneaked forward like silent lizards, pouncing on him, snatching away his rifle. I saw that the captured man was Humpy Jerry, a half-brother of Captain Jack. He didn't offer any resistance.

'Where's Jack?' I asked him.

He hesitated, then pointed his gnarled finger at some large rocks at the edge of the creek.

'He no surrender unless you promise not to hang him,' he said.

Captain Hardeman had listened to the conversation. He stared into Humpy Jerry's grimy face and said, 'Tell Jack he won't be hanged if he gives up now.'

Before I could stop him, Humpy Jerry, who understood some English, cupped his hands to his mouth and yelled out the message.

I glared at Hardeman. 'You had no right to give that assurance,' I snapped. 'You know it's a lie!'

He nodded, unrepentant. 'There's no going back now, Mister Riddle!'

Humpy Jerry's shouted words had

brought an immediate response. Two squaws appeared from the rocks. They were Jack's wives. For a moment they stood clinging to each other for support, blinking, as if unaccustomed to the bright sunshine. They glanced around, afraid of the soldiers.

Then, suddenly, Jack stepped from the rocks, carrying his four-year-old daughter. In the crook of his arm was a rifle. He was wearing Canby's brass-buttoned coat, torn to tatters by rock and thorn.

'Is this really Jack?' Hardeman whispered hoarsely.

'It's him,' I murmured, suddenly filled with misgiving.

Soldiers stood around, hardly able to believe that the Indian who had defied the army for so long was at last within their grasp.

Jack moved his head, his gaze aloof as he viewed his captors, then his eyes found mine and gave a faint glint of recognition. He walked over to me.

'Where's Fairchild?' he asked.

'Not here, Jack,' I said.

'Then I will give my rifle to you,' and he held out the weapon and I grasped it. 'Jack run no more,' he said simply. 'His legs give out.'

All I could say was nothing.

Hardeman was not dumbstruck. He unleashed a cheer of delight, pulled off his campaign hat and threw it in the air. Soon his men were doing the same, yelling out in triumph.

More Indians were emerging from the trees, hands held high . . . Barncho, Slolux and others. They came nervously forward, laying down their weapons.

The war was over.

★ ★ ★

Messengers galloped ahead with the news of Jack's surrender, but the main column's journey back to camp, that warm Sunday afternoon, was made at a leisurely pace. There was no need any longer for haste.

To the soldiers, Jack was fascinating

and awesome. I saw men reach out to touch him, just so they could say they'd done it. He held himself aloof. He'd stood out against the might of the US Army for nearly six months. He'd not betrayed his people, but his people had betrayed him. He was not bound. He sat upright in his saddle, apparently blind to the antics of those around him, his face expressionless except for once, when his gaze fell upon Hooker Jim and his lips formed an ugly Modoc word.

In the evening, as we approached Peninsula Camp, men rushed from their tents and lined the trail, cheering and waving their hats, all anxious to get a glimpse of our captives.

As we entered the camp, a hammering sound bludgeoned our ears. They were already building a gallows for Jack. He remained unmoved, seemingly in his own dream-world.

Our cavalcade halted at the colonel's tent. Davis appeared in full-dress uniform, his face as solemn as a rock.

He spoke directly to Jack — four sharp words: 'Remove General Canby's coat!'

When this was done, matters were not delayed. Under heavy escort, the Modoc ringleaders were marched to the blacksmith's. Here, ready-prepared leg-shackles were fitted. Jack and John Schonchin were chained together and for the first time Jack showed emotion. 'When I give up,' he shouted angrily, 'nobody tell me about chains!'

He achieved nothing. The other Indians were also chained in pairs.

Davis was the most ruthless officer I ever knew. He intended making this the final, short chapter of the war. He had everything planned down to the smallest detail.

As the gallows were erected, the Modoc ringleaders remained in a makeshift compound, chained to stakes and heavily guarded. For some strange reason, Davis showed an act of mercy by permitting Jack's young wife Lizzie and his little daughter to stay with him.

That first night, the Warm Springs Indians staged a great victory dance. In the light of blazing camp-fires, they acted out the war's main incidents, every event accompanied by war-whoops and drumbeats. The audience, made up of soldiers, civilians and even some Modocs watched in fascination. The horror of the past seemed to be forgotten, for many laughed and applauded.

Sickened by the pantomime, I walked to the compound where Jack and his ringleaders were held. I made no attempt to enter, but in the moon's pale light, I saw them chained up, slumped and silent.

I left the compound and walked towards the bluff, but soon came upon the strange sight of a man leaning his weight against the trunk of a cotton-wood tree, shaking it vigorously. As I approached, he stopped. I recognized him. He was a newspaper reporter. 'Damned lazy bird!' he exclaimed.

'What bird?' I asked.

He wiped his brow with the back of his hand. 'Carrier-pigeon,' he said angrily. 'Best way to get my report on Jack's capture to head office, so I thought. But for the last hour all he's done is perch in this bloody tree. Say, can you lend me a hand?'

'Sure,' I said, and we labored at the cottonwood, nigh shaking it from its roots, and presently the flap of wings sounded and we knew the bird was on its way, disappearing into the darkness.

The newspaper-man thanked me. 'One day,' he gasped, 'we'll share a pigeon-pie!'

I climbed to the top of the bluff, welcoming the solitude. I tried to reason some sense into this whole damned war and into the path I was following. I had set out to try and prevent bloodshed, to attempt to bring peace to Toby's people. It seemed to me that I had failed in all respects. All I could do was long for the day when we could settle down at home with life back to normal. But could it ever be normal after the nightmares we'd lived through?

Presently I found a smooth rock, lay down and tried to rest, but my troubled mind prevented me from sleep.

★ ★ ★

Davis was determined to proceed with the executions, believing that this was the best way to finish matters once and for all. Next morning, I accompanied him, with a group of officers, to the compound.

The prisoners were made to stand up, their chains clinking.

Davis launched into his tirade, pausing as I translated:

'Even among your Indian neighbors, the Modocs are known as a tyrannical tribe. As many as three-hundred murders have been committed by your people. The Modocs have never been punished for these crimes.'

Jack looked at the ground, giving no indication as to whether the words were sinking in, but John Schonchin, chained to him, watched us with frightened eyes.

'Regardless of your acts of treachery,' Davis went on, 'the government offered you a reservation of land for a home, where, if you chose, you could have enjoyed the annual bounties of the government. But your band preferred the warpath. You spurned the kindness of the government. And worst of all: you lured General Canby and the peace-commissioners into a trap. They came to make peace and you murdered them.'

Davis now spoke directly to Jack, dropping his voice so that it came low and without mercy.

'I must inform you that I have this day directed that you and your six confederates will be executed at sunset tomorrow.'

For the first time, Jack looked up, met the colonel's pale eyes. He belched. He made no comment. Davis turned and walked briskly from the compound.

Together with the other officers, I followed him.

Suddenly he stopped and faced me. We were standing within sight of the newly erected gallows. Seven nooses had been prepared and workmen were testing the ropes.

'I take no pleasure in this,' Davis said. 'Jack knew he would hang. He knew that as soon as he'd killed General Canby.'

At that moment, the colonel's aide-de-camp spoke up. 'Colonel, sir, there is a courier for you!'

We turned to see the messenger ride up. Reining in his horse before the colonel, he saluted and passed down an envelope. Davis opened it, took out the contents. I saw the color rising in his cheeks as he read. In anger, he crumpled the paper into a ball.

Without a word he stomped off towards his headquarters, his officers hard on his heels, but I stayed behind.

The courier was well aware of the message he'd delivered. 'He's just received orders from Washington,' he said. 'He's not to carry out the executions. The Modocs are to be moved to Fort Klamath to face formal trial.'

18

For a time, Toby and I imagined that the past might slip away and allow us to live in peace. But it was a fool's dream. Just three weeks after our return home, I received an official-looking envelope. I tore it open.

The presence of Frank and Toby Riddle was requested at Fort Klamath. A Military Commission had been appointed for the trial, commencing Tuesday, July 1st, of the Modoc Indians.

Not only were we key witnesses, we were also needed to act as interpreters with payment at ten dollars per day.

That late June day of 1873, we set out to face whatever destiny had in store.

The land had not yet lost its spring freshness. We crossed many rivulets where the water was clear as crystal. We crossed the Siskiyou Mountains, following the road through sweet-smelling pine. We approached Fort Klamath in the mid-morning and gazed at the white-timbered buildings and large parade-ground. Behind the fort rose the snow peaks of the Cascades.

The military post was bustling as we rode in. Showing my letter to an orderly, we were taken straight to the Commanding Officer's office. Captain Robert Pollock was a thick-set man in his forties. His manner was cheerful despite the fact that the heat seemed to be troubling him.

'I trust your stay here will be comfortable,' he said. 'Your room is in the officers' lines. Of course you can come and go as you please, but you must not associate with any of the defendants.'

'Who exactly is standing trial, Captain?' I asked.

'Captain Jack, John Schonchin, Boston Charley, Black Jim, Barncho and Slolux. All those involved in

General Canby's murder.'

'But not Hooker Jim and Bogus?'

'No. The government has confirmed that they are not to be prosecuted.'

'What's going to happen to the rest of the prisoners?' I asked.

'In due course, they will be transported to a reservation at Quapaw in Oklahoma. We hope this will be the end of the trouble.'

After we left Pollock, we turned our horses into the corral and were shown to our accommodation that overlooked the parade-ground. Later, we wandered through the fort and soon found the stockade that housed those Modocs who were prisoners-of-war. In all, at this time, there were some one hundred fifty men, women and children being held.

The stockade had been divided in two to keep the Hot Creek and Lost River Modocs apart and prevent them from squabbling. Guards paced to and fro along raised platforms at the corners of the stockade.

I didn't stay inside the stockade for long, but Toby lingered to chat with a cousin. As I waited for her outside, somebody said, 'Riddle!' and suddenly I was confronted by a smiling Bogus, and before I realized it my hand was being pumped up and down. He was wearing a blue chequered shirt and Levis, and with his pale skin, he looked more like a cowboy than an Indian.

'All Modocs have been moved from Peninsula to here,' he said.

'Do you have to stay in the stockade?' I asked him.

He shook his head. 'Me, Hooker Jim, Shacknasty Jim and Steamboat Frank have our own tents. We're allowed to gamble much as we want. Scarfaced Charley also free, but all he does is sulk.'

'Where's Jack?' I asked.

Bogus pointed to the post guardhouse. I could see a sentry pacing up and down on the porch. 'Every day a lot of settlers come to have a look at Jack. Sometimes they line up outside the guard-house and go in one by one.'

'Is he still chained to John Schonchin?' I asked.

Bogus nodded. 'Chains won't come off till the day they hang him.'

* * *

The trial opened four days later, and was held in the Post Adjutant's office. The military commission consisted of Colonel Elliott as President, and four other officers. All wore full-dress uniform and took their places at the long table. The Judge Advocate was a Major Curtis. Toby and I, feeling tense and uneasy, were given seats on his right. To his left was the court reporter, Doctor Belden, who, I'd heard, could write with the speed of lightning. Everybody looked solemn.

Four soldiers, gripping bayoneted rifles, stood guard.

Suddenly the door opened, and the four bloodhounds — Hooker Jim, Bogus, Steamboat Frank, Shacknasty

Jim — filed in and sat on a bench. The only other persons present were the four ushers.

Colonel Elliott asked that the prisoners be brought in, and we heard outside voices calling, the clinking of chain and shuffling footsteps on the porch boards.

Jack was the first to enter, followed by John Schonchin, the shackle linking them so short they stumbled against each other. Boston Charley and Black Jim, no longer shackled, came in next, and the four were made to sit on a bench. Then came Barncho and Slolux, looking totally unconcerned about the proceedings. They squatted on the floor in front of the others. All six were wearing cotton shirts and blue army trousers. Confinement and lack of fresh air had affected them badly. They had lost weight, were gaunt-looking and weak.

Pompously, Major Curtis read out the order convening the Commission and I interpreted this to the prisoners, though they showed little interest. The members of the Commission and Judge Advocate were then sworn in. After this, both Toby and I were sworn in.

The prisoners were made to stand while the charges were read out. *The murder in violation of the laws of war, of General E.R.S. Canby and Doctor Eleazer Thomas. Attempts to kill A.B. Meacham, L.S. Dyar and T.F. Riddle.*

The prisoners jointly pleaded not guilty to all charges.

I was called upon to testify and the Judge Advocate questioned me. I confirmed the date of Canby's murder, and also that the prisoners now before us were present on that day. He asked me if Captain Jack was the principal man in the tribe, and I said, 'Yes.' He went on to question me about fore-knowledge of the murders, about the warnings I had given to Canby and the peace commissioners, and about events at the peace-tent.

The questions dragged on as other members of the commission took their turn. Everything was translated by Toby for the benefit of the prisoners. At last the questions dried up. The prisoners were asked if they wished to cross-examine the witness. They all shook their heads and I thankfully stood down.

Toby was next called, and I took over the translating. She was questioned in detail about events, and answered clearly, covering much the same ground as me.

L.S. Dyar was next sworn in. He spoke up about his experience as an Indian Agent, and how, with Alfred Meacham, he had worked to get the Modocs onto the reservation. When he stepped down, proceedings were adjourned till the next day and the prisoners were led out.

Over the next two days, the trial continued. Shacknasty Jim, Steamboat Frank, and Hooker Jim were questioned, being only too happy to tell all they knew now that they were safe from hanging themselves.

On the third day, Weium, the Modoc

who had first warned Toby of the intended murders, was under examination when the courtroom door opened, and to our surprise Alfred Meacham stepped quietly in and sat down. He was leaning heavily on a stick, and was clearly still suffering from his injuries, but this didn't prevent him from smoking his pipe. The prisoners gazed at him incredulously. Meacham did not flinch from Jack's gaze until the chief, from his shackled position, offered to shake hands. Only then did Meacham turn his attention elsewhere.

Later, Meacham was called to give evidence, during which both Barncho and Slolux dozed off. Meacham was questioned about his role as Chairman of the Commissioners, of his horrific experiences on the day of the murders. He replied in a firm voice.

In the afternoon, more witnesses for the prosecution were called. At no time, during the entire proceedings, did the Modocs question any evidence given.

On the following day, Scarfaced

Charley, Dave, One-Eyed Moose and several other Modocs testified for the defense. But they had been given no legal guidance and their evidence did nothing for the cause of the defendants.

That afternoon, the Judge Advocate invited Jack to make a statement.

With some difficulty Jack stood up. He looked down at the chains on his legs and said, 'I cannot talk dressed in these chains. My heart is not strong when chains are on my legs.'

I translated but nobody reacted.

The Judge Advocate showed a rare compassion. 'Talk exactly as if you were at home, in a council.'

The room's atmosphere had become taut. Jack raised his dark eyes, his face touched by a fleeting defiance. His voice came more loudly now. He paused impatiently as I translated.

'I see that I have no show, my days are gone. When I was a boy, I had it in my heart to be a friend of the white people. I am not afraid to die, but I am ashamed to die the way that you intend, choked to death. I see no crime in my heart, although I killed Canby. I was forced to do it.'

He paused, collecting his thoughts.

'You white people have driven me from the mountains and valleys. At last you have got me here. I do not think that we should be the only men condemned to die.' He raised an accusing finger towards Hooker Jim and the other turncoats. 'Those men who are free today should surely be with us. Hooker Jim started the killing.

'I hope the white people will not treat my people badly. They are not to blame for the things I did. I am very angry. Many of my people have been murdered by the whites, but not one white man has been punished. I charge the white people with many murders. Think of Ben Wright. The white people in Yreka made a hero of him. Now here I am. I killed one white man after I had been fooled many times. The law says, 'You must hang. You are only an Indian.' Why did not the white man's law say Ben Wright must hang?'

He glanced around the room, but nobody met his eye.

'I have no more words,' he said. 'In a few days I will be no more. You white people didn't conquer me. My own men did.'

After Jack sat down, each of the defendants spoke his piece, apart from Barncho and Slolux who had nothing to say. There was a growing impatience among the members of the commission to get things over.

Afterwards, the Judge Advocate spoke briefly, denying the accusations made by Jack, after which the court was adjourned for members to consider the verdict and sentence. Their findings would be announced next day.

The following morning, we were in court as proceedings were reconvened. The prisoners were brought in and remained standing while Colonel Elliott announced the verdict.

The six defendants had been found guilty on all accounts. All six were sentenced to be hanged.

I translated the sentence to the prisoners, although they'd understood without interpretation, except maybe Barncho and Slolux who looked completely bored. None of the six revealed any emotion as they were led back to their guardhouse cells.

★ ★ ★

'Frank,' Meacham said, reaching out to grip my sleeve, 'I want to ask you a favor.'

It was evening and we were sitting in our room in officers' row. Meacham was leaving early in the morning and had called round to say good-bye and speak to me about a matter in his mind.

'I've always tried to be a worthy Christian,' he went on, 'but I believe I've failed in my duties. Jack has indicated that he wants my forgiveness, my friendship. He offered to shake my hand and I turned away from him. I want to go to him and make amends. I also wish him to know what I plan to do for his people.'

I nodded, sensing what he was contemplating.

He said, 'I'd like you to come with me to visit Jack and translate my words.'

An hour later Meacham and I entered the white-washed guardhouse. Its windows were barred with iron. We were expected, for one of the guards led us straight in. The sergeant of the guard unlocked an inner-door and we went through. So closely packed were the prisoners, that it was difficult to avoid treading on them. The cell was very small. Seven Modocs sat with their backs against the walls, their legs manacled. They sat with their chins on their knees. Stepping between them, the sergeant led us to an adjoining cell. Keys rattled and the cell door swung open. Jack and John Schonchin had been sprawled on the floor, asleep. Jack immediately awoke, looking at us with dull and heavy eyes. John Schonchin remained asleep, snoring softly.

'Jack' Meacham said, 'I've come to shake your hand. I bear you no ill-will for what has happened.'

For a moment Jack seemed completely taken aback by Meacham's words, then suddenly he reached out and shook first Meacham's extended hand, then mine.

We sat down on the floor, wedged close through lack of space.

'Will we die?' Jack asked. 'Or maybe we still have a chance?'

Meacham spoke and I translated. 'You have many friends in the East, Jack. A religious group is trying very hard to help you. People are signing petitions. In the end it will be President Grant who will decide your fate.' He paused, reached out and again took Jack's hand in his. 'But you must not build your hopes too high. You must ask God for forgiveness and prepare yourself for the next world.'

'This next world!' Jack snorted. 'The Sunday Doctor came to see me. He told about the next world, that I had nothing to fear because it was a wonderful place. So I say to him, 'If it's so good, I will exchange places with you. You can go instead of me.' But he wouldn't do it.'

And then Jack did something unexpected. He grinned. And just for a moment the three of us laughed together.

'Jack,' Meacham went on, 'whatever happens, I'm going to write a book and explain all the things that went wrong, that it wasn't all the fault of the Indians. And I'm planning a lecture tour of the East. I want to make people aware of how badly the Modocs have been treated — and how brave they were. I hope to take some Indians with me.'

'Take me,' Jack said brightly.

'If I am allowed to,' Meacham assured him, 'I'll gladly do that.'

Jack nodded. He knew we were playing with words.

'I know we all have to go over the hill

one day, and we will find a good place,' he murmured. 'For some it is sooner than others.'

We could hear the clatter of tins. The prisoners were about to be fed.

'Good-bye, Jack,' Meacham said, his voice hushed. 'We will pray for you.'

We rose, and each shook his hand in a long shake. I knew that Jack's talk about 'going over the hill' didn't mean much. He believed, like all Modocs, that if a man died at the end of a rope, his spirit got suffocated and was unable to escape to the after-life.

When we walked from that dreary place, our hearts were in our boots.

19

In those remaining days of summer I worked hard at our ranch. Even so, my mind was never far from the goings-on at Fort Klamath. The thought of the prisoners, caged in tiny, airless cells, shackled and denied all dignity, robbed my life of any joy.

The weeks slipped by. In late August we had visit from John Fairchild. I showed him some new cows I'd bought. Afterwards we leaned against a fence and smoked our pipes.

'The President has approved the court findings,' he told me. 'They've set the date for the executions — Oct 3.'

'They've got just six weeks left,' I sighed. 'How's Jack standing up to the strain?'

'Apparently he eats scarcely anything. His body's palsied and his hands shake. They're dosing him with opiates.'

'They'll never take his pride away,' I said and we turned and walked back to the cabin in silence.

A week letter I got a letter and it gave me an unpleasant jolt.

'You gone awful pale,' Toby told me.

I held up the letter. 'Just before Jack and the rest of them are hung, the Post Adjutant is going to read them the findings of the military commission and the orders of President Grant. They want me to do the interpreting.'

Toby didn't comment. I put my arm around her shoulder. In my mind was a picture of Jack and the others standing on the scaffold, with ropes around their necks, waiting to die while they listened to meaningless words.

'I don't care what the pay is,' I said. 'I won't do it.'

Through the hot, restless nights of September, a thought grew in me, like some sort of canker. I knew now there was nothing I could do to help Jack and maybe it was some sort of penance, but the thing wouldn't rest in me. I decided

I had to be close to him when he died.

Toby felt too ill to come with me. Her face was full of sadness as I left her on the last day of September and started on horseback for Fort Klamath. I took my time, sleeping out beneath the stars, breathing the fresh, clear air — and all the while comparing it with conditions in a prison cell.

As I neared the fort, the road was crowded with settlers converging for the spectacle of the hangings. Excitement didn't often come to their dull lives.

Next day, October 3, I stood in the crowded meadow and watched the sun lift into the sky, spilling a golden haze over the surrounding mountains. It occurred to me how wonderful it was to be alive and see such beauty.

More settlers had poured into the fort, and many Klamath Indians had come from the reservation to witness the hangings. I also recognized Modocs from Yainax.

The scaffold loomed before us like a dark monster. A ladder led up to the long rectangular platform, and six nooses dangled above the trap. Nearby, heaped earth showed where open graves awaited.

At nine o'clock, with the sun growing warm, a murmur of excitement cut through the crowd. Mounted troops, a band and an empty wagon were lining up on the parade ground. Shortly, they moved to the guardhouse and halted before it.

Around me, people waited, craning their necks to get a first glimpse of the condemned men.

Suddenly there was a gasp as the prisoners emerged and were helped into the wagon. At that moment we heard the cries of Modoc women who were watching from the stockade.

The procession moved slowly towards the gallows with drums muffled and the band playing *The Death March*. As they drew closer, I got a clearer view of the prisoners. Boston Charley and Black Jim were dressed in old army trousers and blouses and were sitting in the front of the wagon, and behind them were Jack and John Schonchin. At the back were Barncho and Slolux.

'They're sittin' on their own coffins,' a man standing next to me whispered, ''ceptin' Barncho and Slolux.'

Jack had a blanket drawn up to his ears. As they halted, Boston, looking more dwarf-like than ever, leaned forward, peering with strange fascination at the gallows. The soldiers formed a three-sided square, while the adjutant stood facing the scaffold. Colonel Wheaton, who was once again in command, took up position behind him. On his left were two officers I didn't recognize. The Officer of the Day, Captain Hoge, stood with his arms folded, and on the scaffold four enlisted men waited behind chairs soon to be filled by the prisoners.

For a moment my gaze drifted away from the scaffold. I saw Scarfaced Charley sitting alone with his back against a tree, his head slumped. And off to the left, occupying a privileged viewpoint, were Hooker Jim and the other three turncoats.

Colonel Wheaton stepped forward and motioned Barncho and Slolux to stay in the wagon. The other four men were helped to the ground.

Jack's blanket had slipped away. He was wearing a striped cotton shirt. His eyes were sunken deep into black sockets, but as his glance swept around the crowd, there was no fear in his gaunt face. He stood patiently as the chains were chiseled free of his legs and those of the other prisoners, after which the four were forced to climb onto the scaffold platform.

Jack and Black Jim showed no emotion as each man was assigned a chair beneath a noose. Boston Charley chewed on a cud of baccy. John Schonchin looked dizzy and almost fell as he reached his chair.

The adjutant followed them onto the scaffold, and when all were sitting he read aloud the official order for execution. This was interpreted by Dave Hill, who had taken on the job I'd refused. When he'd finished, the adjutant slipped another piece of paper from his pocket and again read aloud.

The executive order dated August 22 1873 approving sentence of certain Modoc Indian prisoners is hereby modified in the case of Barncho and Slolux and the sentence in said cases is commuted to imprisonment for life.
Signed
U.S. GRANT-President

Dave Hill made clear the meaning of the words to Slolux and Barncho. They sat down on the coffins but showed no joy at their reprieve. They seemed bewildered by everything.

A chaplain climbed onto the scaffold. Quietly, he read from a Bible. When he'd finished, Captain Hoge walked to a bucket of water and quenched his thirst. He then ordered a corporal to offer water to the condemned men.

Black Jim and Boston Charley each swallowed a mouthful, but Jack and John Schonchin shook their heads.

The limbs of the condemned men were bound and the ropes fitted around their necks, then black hoods were placed over their heads. They were ordered to stand up and the chairs were removed. I noticed a corporal with an axe standing by the rope that held the trap. The chaplain offered up a brief prayer. As he made the sign of the cross, the Officer of the Day raised a white handkerchief and the corporal's axe flashed in the sunlight. The trap collapsed with an earth-shaking thump.

Four bodies were dangling in the air.

Suddenly, the Modocs watching from the stockade unleashed an anguished, keening wail — a sound that rose higher and higher, drowning out all other sound.

I took one last glimpse at the scaffold, saw the bodies of Jack and Black Jim swinging easily, but Boston and John Schonchin were still gripped by terrible convulsions.

I turned and pushed myself out of the gabbling crowd. I ran from the meadow and away from the fort. I stood alone in the quiet pines. I felt in need of a strong drink, but there was none. I found a stream and dipped my face and hands in it. If Hooker Jim hadn't talked Jack into killing Canby, other, more deserving corpses would be swinging on those ropes.

Jack had paid the penalty because he was chief, because he had allowed himself to be pushed into the rash deed of murder. His loyalty had always been to his people, and he had always kept his word. Before the whites had come, the Modocs lived in harmony with their surroundings. But then miners and settlers had poured in and turned everything upside down. I was as much to blame as anybody. Jack had fought a lonely battle to hold onto his land. He'd fought as any decent man would've done. But his death was the price that had to be paid for peace.

Hours later, I walked back to the fort. The crowds had left. Workmen were dismantling the scaffold, but the graves still remained empty.

I wandered through the army buildings. I came upon a large tent and was about to pass it when I happened to glance through its open flap.

In the tent's center stood a long table, covered by a black, rubber sheet. Around it, Doctor McElderry was working with two assistants. All were wearing blood stained aprons. Four corpses were stretched out on the table. The scene was bathed in a lantern's yellow light. It was like a picture painted by the Devil.

For a moment nobody knew I was there. I saw McElderry laboring with a surgical-saw. He grunted with satisfaction as he completed his task. Next, he lifted the object he had separated, held it up in the light for a moment, then placed it on a side table . . . it was Jack's head!

McElderry looked up, saw me.

'Mister Riddle!' he exclaimed. 'You startled me.'

He followed my gaze to the bloody object on the side table. He gestured with his hands. 'Heads are to be shipped to the Surgeon General in Washington,' he said. 'I've got to scrape out all the soft parts and pack them in a barrel. All in the interest of medical science!'

I backed from the tent, wordless and sickened.

20

'Plenty of folks will try to set down what happened in the Modoc War,' Alfred Meacham, still frail, told me when he visited our ranch the following summer. 'And most of them, one way or another, will get it wrong.'

Toby was sitting with us at the supper-table, her eyes bright with excitement at Meacham's visit. She'd put on some weight these past years but her face was as pretty as it had been on the first day I saw her.

Meacham removed the pipe from his lips and smiled. 'We survived. That's what makes us so important. And you, Frank, were the best eyewitness of all. Now it's up to you to make everybody understand what it was really like - how the Modocs merely reacted to years of provocation.'

I pondered on his words. 'I guess,' I

said, 'the Modoc War is typical of what's happening to all the Western tribes. We've got to somehow stop this constant pressure building up against the Indians.'

'Sure,' he nodded. 'While the Indians are continually pushed out by so-called manifest destiny, war will surely follow. The whole concept of Indian policy must be reformed. That's why I'm going to tour the East and speak my mind. I want people to realize that whites don't have a God-given right to racial superiority.'

'After the treatment the Modocs gave you,' I said, 'how can you feel this way?'

He took a deep breath. For a moment, it was as if he was already on his platform. 'Because I believe that win or lose, war and honor are incompatible.' He gave me a droll smile. 'Folks'll reckon that as the Good Lord has allowed me to live, despite being shot seven times, nigh scalped and having half my ear sliced off, I must have something worthwhile to tell. And to add color, I want to take along some Modocs. I want you and Toby to come too. To translate the words, to tell your story alongside mine. First thing is to see if Scarfaced Charley and some others will come East.'

He leaned back in his chair, his eyes glowing with enthusiasm. 'Frank,' he said, 'will you and Toby help me?'

Toby couldn't hold back her eagerness. 'Sure we help you,' she said.

So it was that one month later Meacham and I got off the train at Seneca, Oklahoma, and traveled in a buggy along a dirt road to the Quapaw Agency. I was weary after our long journey, but Meacham seemed a new man. It was a warm day, and the land was flat and dry, though greener than California.

Soon after the executions, the remaining Modoc prisoners, some hundred fifty men, women and children, had been transported two-thousand miles by wagons and railroad boxcars to this their new home. The Government

241

had banned them from California for ever. With Jack gone, Scarfaced Charley had become chief. Now, the Indians were settling in to log cabins.

As we got closer, Meacham shaded his eyes from the sun and squinted hard. 'Bless me!' he exclaimed. 'That sure is the strangest sight I ever did see.'

I followed his gaze to a meadow that fronted the cabins. Four Indians were playing some sort of game, knocking a ball through hoops with long-handled mallets.

'Croquet,' Meacham explained. 'Who ever dreamed we'd find Hooker Jim, Scarfaced Charley, Steamboat Frank and Shacknasty Jim playing croquet?'

It was a surprising sight, but even more surprising was Meacham himself. I marveled at him. His health and spirit were improving every day. Passion for his projects had given him the will to recover.

The Modocs spotted us, called out in joyful voices and a moment later were embracing us and pumping our hands like bosom pals, even Hooker Jim, though the touch of his leathery shake was something that turned my stomach.

Soon we were joining in the game. We tapped the wooden ball through the hoops. For a while we laughed a lot, and pretended that the past had never happened.

But eventually Scarfaced Charley complained about how the Quapaw Agent wanted the Modocs to give up their language. At the agency school, the children would be taught only English. They would not be allowed to practice their Indian ways.

Scarfaced Charley said, 'They want to blow our Modoc spirit away in the wind.'

'That's why we're here,' Meacham said. 'We want to save the Modoc culture before it's too late.'

And then he explained how he intended to do it.

After he'd finished, Scarfaced Charley, Shacknasty Jim and Steamboat Frank were tickled pink by the idea of seeing the big cities in the East. They'd gladly travel on a lecture-tour when Meacham sent for them. But Hooker Jim lowered his eyes and shook his head. He was still scared that somebody would single him out for vengeance.

When Meacham and I eventually left Quapaw, we were in good spirits.

'What we've experienced,' Meacham was saying, 'and what we've suffered, wasn't in vain. No matter what you think of yourself, Frank, you're a brave man. And you're the linking thread that's vital if my dream's to come true - a dream to draw some purpose, some good, from the shambles of this war.' He paused for a moment, and then in a quiet voice he added: 'We must prepare ourselves to go on tour by next spring. God willing, we can bring about a better understanding between whites and Indians.'

A TOWN CALLED
TROUBLESOME

John Dyson

Matt Matthews had carved his ranch out of the wild Wyoming frontier. But he had his troubles. The big blow of '86 was catastrophic, with dead beeves littering the plains, and the oncoming winter presaged worse. On top of this, a gang of desperadoes had moved into the Snake River valley, killing, raping and rustling. All Matt can do is to take on the killers single-handed. But will he escape the hail of lead?